CHRISTMAS

JARS

Reunion

CHRISTMAS JARS Reunion

A NOVEL

JASON F. WRIGHT

SHADOW
MOUNTAIN

For my brothers, Sterling and Jeff,
and for my favorite sister, Terilynne

First printing in hardbound 2009
First printing in paperbound 2011

Visit us at ShadowMountain.com

Library of Congress Cataloging-in-Publication Data

Wright, Jason F.
  Christmas jars reunion / Jason F. Wright.
      p. cm.
  ISBN 978-1-60641-165-0 (hardbound : alk. paper)
  ISBN 978-1-60641-849-9 (paperbound)
  1. Church charities—Fiction. I. Title.
  PS3623.R539C484 2009
  813'.6—dc22   2009022747

Printed in the United States of America
Publishers Printing, Salt Lake City, UT

10   9   8   7   6   5   4   3   2   1

ACKNOWLEDGMENTS

Love, thanks, and chocolate to my wife and eternal companion, Kodi. Much appreciation also to my children: Oakli Shane, Jadi Thompson, Kason Samuel, and Koleson Ward. They fill my jar more than I could ever fill theirs.

Far too often I overlook an important group when the time comes to draft a pithy *thank you* for the very page you're reading. They are the wonderful booksellers across the country who embrace small books not necessarily on the national radar. The original *Christmas Jars* was just such a book, but because of the spirit and tenacity of booksellers, it eventually became a *New York Times* bestseller and the vehicle for a holiday tradition that has become far bigger and more important than the book itself. So to the booksellers at our cozy and beloved independents, chain bookstores large and small, big box retailers, and to the

Internet pioneers, I say *thank you.* Without you the *Christmas Jars* movement would still be just a flicker, and not the brush-fire of goodwill it has become since 2005.

Thank you to Chris Schoebinger, Sheri Dew, and their gifted colleagues at Shadow Mountain for carrying the torch so nobly and for so long.

A very special nod to those who have welcomed me with open arms into their homes, churches, schools, and community events to discuss the *Giving Gene* and to share in the *Spirit of the Jar.* You are also responsible for this movement becoming about much more than a simple book.

Finally, I remain in awe of the thousands of people who have read *Christmas Jars, Christmas Jars Reunion,* or *Penny's Christmas Jar Miracle* and, as a result, have started jars of their own. This year in a beautifully unorganized way, millions of dollars in spare change will be given away during the days leading up to Christmas. That is nothing less than a modern-day miracle.

A note about the chapter headings:

The quotes at the beginning of each chapter are excerpts from actual e-mails received from readers across the country. They are identified by first name only to protect the magic of the *Spirit of the Jar.* They are used by permission.

Many other true stories of Christmas Jar miracles can be read online at http://www.ChristmasJars.com, where you are also invited to share your own miracle.

PROLOGUE

From Christmas Jars

Louise Jensen was sitting alone, licking her fingers two at a time and paying serious attention to her greasy chicken-leg-and-thigh platter, when she heard muffled crying from the booth behind her at Chuck's Chicken 'n' Biscuits on U.S. Highway 4. It was early Friday afternoon. It was also New Year's Eve.

Although discovering an unattended, blue-eyed, newborn baby girl was not on her list of expectations, Louise was the faithful brand of woman who believed that everything happened for a reason. She reached down and lifted the pinkish baby into her arms. Tucked inside a stained elephant blanket, near the baby's neck, she found an unsigned, handwritten note:

To the next person to hold my baby girl,
She is yours now. I'll miss her more than you know. But I love

her too much to raise her with a daddy that hits. Truth is, he didn't even want me to have her anyways, and her life will be better without a mommy that will always need to run. Please tell her I love her. And please tell her I will hold her again.

I cannot give her much, but this year I give her the life her daddy wouldn't. And a little bit of hope.

It was such magic in our lives. The gift left to us by someone restored something in my family and me. My troubles aren't gone, but MY HOPE is restored.
—JBM

ONE

Twenty-Five Years Later

Chuck might be the only person ever to write his last will and testament on the back of a paper placemat." Preacher Longhurst paused as soft laughter rolled across the crowd assembled under the mammoth green canopy erected in the field behind Chuck's Chicken 'n' Biscuits. "But friends, who are we kidding, there were probably a lot of things Chuck was the first person to ever dream of."

Hope Jensen smiled from her folding chair on the second row.

"And that's why we loved him. It was not just for his secret recipe that produced fried chicken so tasty it could have been made by angels in hairnets, but also for his heavenly Three Musketeers pie, his Sing for a Wing talent nights, and his Cluck Truck that was a rolling landmark around town. Who here hasn't been sitting at a stoplight when Chuck pulled up behind you and all you could see in the rearview mirror was a yellow beak? You'd smile, he'd wave, and if you were lucky, he'd honk the only horn ever manufactured that went 'buck-buck.'"

The congregation laughed, partly for the memory of Chuck's famous horn, but mostly for the silly sound effect Preacher Longhurst made with his lips pressed against the microphone.

Hope looked at Marianne's soft expression and squeezed her hand. Marianne had only known Chuck since she had been reunited with Hope three years earlier, but he'd become family to her, just as the Maxwells had. In fact, he became family to nearly everyone who'd ever had a meal at Chuck's Chicken 'n' Biscuits.

"Friends and neighbors, there was more to Chuck than his sense of humor, and he wasn't just about *customer* service. He was about *people* service. More often than not when you saw the Cluck Truck around the county it meant that Chuck was delivering free meals to schools, church functions, or the seniors' center. His sweetheart, Gayle, tells me he gave away as many meals as he sold during his many years in business."

Gayle nodded from the family section in the front row.

"Dear friends, I know that some among us find it ironic that a preacher from a church Chuck never attended is officiating his funeral. I have wondered the same thing. The truth is that Chuck rarely attended church. I invited him every time I saw him, usually on Sundays for lunch or when I was brave enough to participate in Sing for a Wing night. But his answer never deviated. And these words will sound familiar to his family, I'm sure. He always told me, 'Preacher, just because I'm not in God's house doesn't mean he's not in mine.'"

He looked down at Gayle from the wobbly tabletop pulpit. "Chuck's church was here, wasn't it? Here at the diner, where he did more good for God than any of us will ever know." He reached down to the table and pulled something from a large envelope.

"Now I know this is rather unusual, but this whole day feels different, doesn't it? I've discussed this with Gayle and with her enthusiastic support I'm going to read Chuck's will for you."

Gayle smiled, reaffirming her blessing, and clutched her unopened package of Kleenex. With her eyes closed she saw herself sitting in a booth five years earlier with her husband late one evening. Chuck had suffered a very mild heart attack and was convinced it was time for a will. But instead of hiring an attorney and producing long, complicated lists of wishes, assets, and disclosures, he jotted down his thoughts in tiny letters on the back of a paper placemat. With one hand he wrote, with the other he ate a piece of pie and nursed a carton of chocolate milk.

Hope reached forward and tenderly rubbed Gayle's back.

Gayle's two grown sons, Joel and Mike, sat on her right and left and simultaneously looped their arms through hers.

Preacher Longhurst unfolded the placemat and held it high for the guests to see. Those in the first few rows laughed at the mustache Chuck had sketched on the diner's longtime logo: a cartoon chicken.

"'The one and only will and testament of Charles 'Chuck' Quillon. If you're reading this then I've kicked the chicken bucket.'" Preacher Longhurst looked up and out at the crowd. "It says, 'If read aloud, pause for laughter.'"

They laughed again.

"'If I'm dead, I either choked on a chicken bone, had a heart attack worse than last month's, or Gayle finally made good on her threat to smother me in my sleep and take my vast personal wealth. I hope for the sake of a good story that it was the latter.'"

Hope whispered something in Marianne's ear.

"You're so bad." Marianne poked her in the side.

"'What to do with my stuff.'" Preacher Longhurst looked up again. "You'll have to excuse me, the writing is quite small here." He held the placemat closer to his face. "'My stuff. The restaurant to Gayle and the boys. The red Mustang to my brother, Derrick. The silver-and-black one to Randall, the best cook in America. The stuffed chicken by the register to Eva, the worst waitress in America.'"

Eva laughed loudly and clapped her hands twice in delight.

"'Last. My two certificates of deposit from Southern Family Credit Union. Gayle will cash in and divide equally with everyone who ever worked at Chuck's. Be prepared to be surprised.'" There were several gasps throughout the tent and someone actually clapped. Before long they were all applauding.

Preacher Longhurst continued. "'Rules for my funeral. Number one. No crying. Number two. No church. Funeral must be held at diner or outside in the meadow.'" He smiled and gestured with one hand to the rented tent that sheltered some two hundred guests less than fifty yards from Chuck's. "'Number three. No sad and hokey two-for-one deaths. This isn't some cheesy novel or chick flick. If I go first, Gayle must live for a minimum of twenty more years.'"

The crowd laughed and Gayle rolled her eyes.

"'Number four. No use of the words "mourners," "grief," or "beef."'" Preacher Longhurst shook his head. "I just got that," he said sheepishly.

"'Number five. Serve a free meal before or after. Leg-and-thigh platter with tots. But no free drinks.'"

The crowd laughed even harder.

"'Number six. Everyone gets a jar. Hope's in charge." Preacher Longhurst pointed at a row of banquet tables running along one side of the tent. Covering the tables were Mason jars bearing a black-and-gold label that read *Christmas Jar.*

Gayle turned around and winked at Hope.

Hope glanced at her best friend, Hannah Maxwell, on one side, Marianne on the other, and gave the preacher a thumbs-up.

"'Lastly, number seven. Keep living. Because I'll know if you've stopped.'"

Preacher Longhurst held up the placemat once again and pointed out where Chuck had signed and dated it and reminded everyone that despite its uniqueness, it was, in fact, a legally binding document. He added a few more words of his own about the legacy of Chuck Quillon and closed with a scripture.

Both of Chuck's sons spoke briefly. Then his brother, Derrick, spoke until he began to lose composure. He finished, "I better sit down now before I cry and lose that Mustang."

Finally, Hope, Hannah, and Marianne stood and sang a closing hymn that could have been written by just about anyone in attendance: "Because I Have Been Given Much." There wasn't a dry eye in the tent.

After a benediction by one of Chuck's grandchildren, the pallbearers loaded the plain casket into the hearse and the guests made their way to a small cemetery ten miles south down U.S. Highway 4. There was no graveside service, just a moment or two of private reflection. Many stopped to touch the casket or whisper something kind into the wind.

A team of folks had stayed back at the diner to prepare for lunch so by the time the procession returned, the tent had been filled with tables and chairs and hot chicken and tots were being served on heavy-duty paper plates. Five-gallon coolers bearing Chuck's cartoon chicken logo poured lemonade.

"What a turnout," Hope said to Hannah Maxwell.

"Not surprising though, right? Who in the south hasn't eaten at Chuck's at least once? See that lady over there?" She pointed with her fork to an older woman sitting at the far side of the tent. "That's Terri Alexander. I think she's from Tampa. She heard from a friend of a friend that Chuck passed and wanted to be here."

Hannah repeated the point to her husband, Dustin, and the two began counting how many people in the crowd were unfamiliar to them.

Hope rested her head on Marianne's shoulder for a moment and relaxed. It had been a tiring four days. Chuck died on Thanksgiving evening, alone in the kitchen, after serving free meals to anyone who'd asked. It was an annual tradition at Chuck's, and it seemed natural that he'd leave the earth on the same day he gave several dozen others a full stomach and one more day of life. Gayle said that at age seventy-four, after all that Chuck had accomplished, no one could say that he'd left behind any unfinished songs.

This had been Hope's first funeral since Adam Maxwell's three years earlier when she'd sat shyly in the back. She'd not grown up with a traditional father of her own, but she'd certainly had two terrific dads. Between Adam and Chuck she'd had more love and fatherly guidance than most girls she knew.

Hope looked at Marianne and warmed at the thought that not only had she loved two fathers, but in a strange way, two mothers as well. Raised with such unconditional care by her late mother, Louise, she was now cherished by Marianne. The two were much more like sisters than mother and daughter. In fact, Hope reserved the title of *Mother* only for Louise, even though it was as crystal clear as their stunning eyes that Marianne was Hope's biological mother.

By now practically everyone in the county knew she'd been mentored by Adam for a short time, and by Chuck since birth. She surveyed the funeral scene and proudly wondered how many other people could make such a claim.

Adam's widow, Lauren, had adjusted well to the loss of her

husband. She volunteered at the hospital three days a week and at an elementary school the other two days. The weekends were spent with her grandchildren, recharging her battery, and keeping her mind off the loneliness of a king-sized bed. And because Christmas was just three weeks away, she enjoyed telling people she was "beyond busy" with the Christmas Jars Ministry.

Hope watched as the first wave of people finished lunch and began stopping by the tables to pick up their Christmas Jars. A few spotted Hope at her table, caught her eye, and proudly raised their jars for her to see. She blew them a kiss and waved good-bye.

She knew that everyone would find a rolled-up note, tied with green yarn, inside the jar which explained its purpose:

Thank you for honoring Chuck's wish and taking a Christmas Jar with you. The tradition may already be a familiar one, and if it is and you already have a jar at home, we thank you again and invite you to give this jar to someone who is not yet part of the magic. If this is your introduction to the tradition, we ask you to place this jar on your counter at home, or anywhere it can easily be seen and reached. Each day drop your spare change, coins only, into the jar. On or around Christmas Eve, give the jar away anonymously to someone in need. The need is yours to judge and the decision of who receives the jar is yours and yours alone to make. As soon as possible after Christmas, place a new jar on the counter and begin filling it for next year. The miracle begins with you!

Every time we put change in our jar we will be reminded of the importance of giving to others and to be thankful for what God has blessed us with.

—*Peggy*

TWO

It took ninety minutes for most of the guests to finish their lunches, say their good-byes, and filter out of the tent and back into the unseasonably warm afternoon. More than one person suggested to Gayle, "Chuck must have had something to do with the weather . . ."

Hope and a handful of volunteers began gathering trash and removing the disposable plastic tablecloths. Her eyes met Gayle's across the tent, who was still unable to sit and eat because lingering well-wishers kept coming by to talk to her; it seemed everyone had a story to tell. Watching her, Hope was reminded that with Chuck now gone, Gayle was the only one alive who'd known her every single day of her life, beginning the night she was left by Marianne and discovered by Louise in a booth at the diner next door.

Marianne and her husband, Nick, sat at a table alone and played tic-tac-toe with tater tots on a board Marianne drew on a napkin. They were hardly newlyweds with thirteen years behind them, but they still had the glow of a couple just married and unable to keep their eyes—or hands—off each other. Nick said they still acted like newlyweds because they hadn't ever had a formal honeymoon, and Marianne held out hope one was coming.

If Marianne had been happy when she and Hope first had their tearful reunion, she was electrically ecstatic now. Marianne had easily persuaded Nick to move closer, and he'd come up with the idea to finance a small salon so Marianne could take control over her new career as a hairstylist. Those who knew them suspected Nick opened the salon so he and Marianne could sleep in longer and set their own hours without permission from Marianne's manager at the old salon where she'd learned the trade. Hope didn't care why; she simply loved having Marianne in her life. And after a failed first marriage to Hope's biological, deadbeat father, Marianne deserved all the happiness she and Nick could create.

As long planned, Hannah and Dustin had taken over the Maxwell family furniture restoration business. But Restored wasn't the same without Adam's energy and passion, and though it wasn't yet public knowledge, Hope was sure Hannah and Dustin wouldn't continue the struggle much longer.

What she wasn't as sure of was exactly how she felt about the prospect of Clark Maxwell taking over. Hannah had hinted that Clark, a semipro baseball player and one of Adam's nephews, was considering moving to town to try his hand at keeping the business afloat and in the family.

Hope knew Clark very well. They'd met two years earlier at Sing for a Wing night at Chuck's. Clark and his dad—Adam's brother JJ—were in town visiting Lauren for the first time since Adam's funeral and Clark had created sparks with Hope—both good and bad—during that eight-day visit.

Subsequent visits were no different. Clark would swoop into town for a few days here, a week there, and the chemistry would pop, bubble, and boil over the edge until Clark vanished for a tryout for some minor league baseball team in a town no one but Clark had ever heard of.

He was rumored to arrive for a trial run as the future owner of Restored any day now.

Hope didn't sit down until all that was left to deal with was the empty rented tent, a few chairs that belonged to Chuck's and not the funeral home, and the table and podium Preacher Longhurst had used. She pulled two chairs together, sat in one and propped her feet on the other.

"Hope, you coming to the cemetery?" Clara and Julie, the Maxwell twins, appeared under the tent. "Some of us that stayed back to help with lunch are going over now to pay our respects."

"I think I'll stay for now, thanks though. I'll go later."

"You sure?" Clara asked.

"Yeah—" Hope started.

"Come on." Julie took Hope's right hand and tried to pull her to her feet. "Come with us. There's nothing more to clean up and they're coming soon to take this thing down anyway."

Hope resisted the pull and remained planted firmly in the chair.

In the three years since their father's death, the Maxwell twins had met and married Braden and Tyson Wright, two brothers who had swept into town selling home security systems and never left. The twins were happily married to the Wright brothers and wanted the same joy for Hope. So when they weren't creating trouble or on a double date with their husbands, they were playing matchmaker. They'd set her up on at least a dozen blind dates just that year. Half of them ended awkwardly at the front door, a few ended between dinner and the planned movie, and one infamous date ended after a thirty-seven-minute trip to and from Chick-fil-A. Second dates were unusual.

Julie grabbed Hope's left hand as well and tried again. "Come, come, come. Gayle's gone home for a nap, the brothers are inside the restaurant talking, and most of the grandkids went with Hannah and Dustin to their place."

"Really, I appreciate it," Hope said, "but I'll wait here for the guys to take down the tent. I'm spent. My feet hurt. I'll drive down to the cemetery with Marianne later tonight."

The twins relented, hugged her good-bye, and joined the small group in the parking lot waiting for their turn to visit Chuck's grave.

Hope looked around the empty tent and noticed for the first time how badly they'd trampled the early winter grass. She wondered if Chuck had ever imagined such a showing for his funeral. He would have approved, she decided, of every detail, including his gorgeous seventeen-year-old granddaughter, Lili, with her model-long legs directing funeral traffic while wearing a chicken costume. "Grandpa would want me to," she'd told Gayle that morning. She was right.

Hope stood and walked to the lone remaining table. She gingerly sat on it, holding her breath and testing its weight. Then she tried to slide the portable wooden pulpit away but noticed Preacher Longhurst had left his Bible behind it. She picked up the book, swung her legs around and laid flat on the table. Again she marveled at the warm spell that made December first feel like September first and she pulled at the sides of her black dress, straightening it across her legs. The dress was an expensive luxury she'd bought for herself in New York that summer with Marianne. *I didn't buy this for a funeral,* she thought. Above her heart on the dress she'd pinned a broach Chuck had given her on her twelfth birthday, celebrated like so many of her other birthdays inside the diner.

Staring at the underside of the tent's dirty roof, Hope mentally counted how many people had taken jars. *I think we labeled two hundred and twenty jars,* she thought. *Have we ever placed that many in one day? No chance. I wonder how many people will start filling a jar for this year. It's kinda late, I guess. Still though, maybe a hundred start now? Sure they will. That's less than half that took 'em. So a hundred start today and save . . . how much? Fifty dollars by Christmas? No, too much. That's two dollars a day. No. Maybe a dollar. That's twenty-five dollars in each jar. Twenty-five hundred dollars total saved in jars by Christmas Eve. Not bad at all. And next year? Two hundred jars times . . . hmmm, two hundred dollars maybe? What's that, twenty grand? No . . .*

Hope was much too tired for math. Instead she opened the Bible and began reading from the first verse she saw. Romans 1:4. But the Bible, a warm afternoon, late nights, and grief were enough. By verse eighteen Hope had dozed into a light nap.

Ten minutes later Clark Maxwell pulled into the parking lot at Chuck's Chicken 'n' Biscuits, walked into the funeral tent, and saw what certainly looked like a dead woman in a black dress, lying face up on a table, clutching a Bible with her eyes closed.

*What a surprise. Who would set money outside of our door,
and why? We immediately put a sign on our door saying
"THANK YOU—The gift will go on." Thank you
to our Christmas Angel.*
—Heidi

THREE

Five years in Idaho Falls and Aaron still hated it. The wind
blew eighteen hours a day, and during the quiet hours it was so
cold you wouldn't have known if it was blowing anyway. Your
skin was too numb.

Aaron Albert Allred had lived in six states and burned
through twice that many jobs since being hired out of college at
a commercial insurance agency. He thrived in his early twenties,
always first in, last out, and always out-earning his colleagues.
But after being laid off from a mid-level management position
with California's largest insurance company, "Al," as his few
friends called him, took every penny he'd ever earned—and
much of what his second wife had earned—and invested in an
Internet-based paintball store. It failed. And so did the marriage,
in equally explosive fashion.

Broke and single, Al took a position at a health benefits start-up company, but the CEO didn't appreciate Al making moves on his secretary, who coincidentally happened to be the CEO's wife. Al's choice was simple: walk away or face a sexual harassment complaint with a fat wallet behind it.

He blew the secretary a kiss and drove to the Santa Anita racetrack.

His relationship resume consisted of mostly bad references. He'd been married to or lived with a string of women: once for three years, once for four, once for eight months, and once for just a week shy of five years. The last had been his best effort at an honest, trusting relationship, but his ex-wife met someone younger, richer, and with a smaller belt. Even Al had to recognize karma when she walked out the door one morning carrying a suitcase and wearing a tennis skirt and red lipstick.

Al's temper mellowed through the years, but his penchant for women with a different last name did not. *If nothing else I've always tried,* he convinced himself. *Some guys are just too afraid to take the plunge.* Of course his exes probably would have preferred he never had.

His latest job was in sales and account management, and the flexible schedule and lack of a traditional chain of command suited him. He told his neighbors he was trading in heads of cattle and representing some of the largest ranches in the Western U.S. The truth was that he sold Cowboy Craig's Beef Jerky to convenience stores and gas stations along I-15. His territory stretched from the southern Idaho border north to Butte, Montana.

Al's responsibilities included restocking, invoicing, setting up new displays, and occasionally bartering for more floor or shelf space. What he really wanted to do, though—and he reminded Cowboy Craig at every opportunity—was to help take the highly profitable regional company national. His angle was consistent and relentless: "CC, there's no reason something that works so well on a small scale wouldn't work on a large one."

But Cowboy Craig resisted, insisting the company was exactly the size he wanted. Big enough to provide a nice living for everyone involved, but small enough he knew his clients' names and why they mattered.

Despite their differences of opinion, Al was undeniably good at his job. He had, after all, sold himself as a suitable marital prospect to three different women.

In every other place Al had ever worked, December first meant winter was still weeks away, if coming at all. But in Idaho Falls, the same date meant it was time to write his third rent check of the winter. The area had already endured several snowstorms and there weren't enough layers to battle a wind that whipped like gossip through the small town.

Al woke up early that day. A few weeks earlier the Gas Shack in Pocatello had hired a young, blonde, attractive new morning manager and he was hoping to arrive in the closing moments of her shift to casually invite her to a nice lunch at

Denny's. He dressed in slacks and a tan polo with the Cowboy Craig logo embroidered on the breast. It was an upgrade she couldn't help but notice.

The company warehouse where he parked his cargo van every evening was ten minutes away on the other side of Idaho Falls. "I'm pushing my luck," Al muttered, splashing on the same cologne he'd been wearing for a decade. He quickly put a sweater on over his polo, pulled a coat from the hall closet, put it on and zipped it up, and finished with a scarf around his neck.

"Here we go," he said as he pulled open the front door, twisted the inside door handle lock and slammed it shut before running down the stairs of his apartment complex to his car. The first flight of stairs, completely protected from the elements, was dry and clear. The second flight had small patches of ice leftover from a weekend storm. The third and final flight was more exposed, and he slowed his pace and stepped deliberately over slick patches of dangerous ice.

He reached the sidewalk, well tended by the maintenance crew. "Not today," he smirked as he arrived safely at his car. Then he felt both front pockets for his keys, checked his coat pockets that held the bulky gloves he hated wearing, patted his front pockets again, and cursed.

Al ran back up the stairs, unlocked the door, and spent five minutes scavenging his two-bedroom apartment for his key ring before he remembered. "Pants," he grumbled and fetched his keys from the pocket of yesterday's jeans on the bedroom floor.

He raced back down the stairwell and flew—literally—down the final flight of stairs. Al didn't need a doctor to tell him his left leg was broken.

It could have been twenty below zero and he wouldn't have felt any more pain.

He lay face first on the sidewalk with his palms badly cut and stinging from the salt pellets that had embedded in his skin upon impact. They didn't hurt nearly as much as his lower leg, and the blood dripping into his right eye told him his forehead had been sliced open. He reached up and wiped just above his eyebrow. The blood warmed his fingertips enough to convince him he wasn't dead.

He rolled himself over and squinted into the white sun. The little girl standing beside him had long, brown curly hair and a loud, unafraid voice. She looked six or seven years old and Al thought he'd seen her around the complex.

"Are you OK? Sir?" The girl set down her retro Smurfs lunchbox and knelt beside him. "Sir? Hello? Are you there? Are you alright?"

"My leg is broken, midget." Al covered his face with both hands. "What do you think?"

"Oh! And your hand is bleeding, too. Can I help you?"

"Get your parents."

"I only have a mom."

"Who cares, kid, get her. Get anyone."

The little girl stood. "Wait here," she said before racing

toward her building. It felt like two hours to Al, but just moments later the little girl returned with her mother.

"Oh, my goodness!" the woman said. "Are you OK, Mr. Allred?"

"What is it with you two? I'm on the ground and my leg is on fire. Do you think I'm OK?"

She ignored the question. "I've already called the ambulance. They're coming."

"Fantastic." He wondered if he should be embarrassed that she knew his name while he couldn't have guessed hers if given ten thousand tries. He wasn't.

Al tilted his head to the side and saw the girl's snow boots and her mother's slippers. He closed his eyes. When he reopened them he saw a half-dozen pairs of shoes in his eye-line.

"We're going to load you on a backboard," a male voice said.

"My back is fine."

"It's a precaution."

"My back is *fine*," he repeated and tried to sit up.

"Sir, it's a mandatory precaution," the EMT said much more firmly and motioned for two others to position the board on the ground next to Al.

Al noticed there was a crowd in the parking lot as the EMTs carefully strapped him to the board and placed braces on his leg and neck.

"This is ridiculous," Al protested. "It's my leg, you idiots."

The team lifted and loaded him into the ambulance and drove off.

An Idaho Falls police officer approached the little girl and her mother. "What's your name, dear?"

"My *real* name?"

The female officer smiled and looked at the mother. "Yes, sweetheart, your *real* name."

"Lara. L-a-r-a. There's no *u* sound. But Mommy calls me Queen Lara. Or Queen. Or sometimes Lara Q. Or when she's mad she—"

"OK, Lara, that's enough," her mother said, rolling her eyes. "I'm Laura, too." She extended her hand to the police officer. "Traditional spelling, including the U."

"Really?" the officer asked, puzzled.

"Long story."

"So Lara, did you see what happened to the man?"

"Yes, Officer, yes I did. I was coming to the car. I missed the bus because Mom overslept. . . . She works a lot," she whispered. "I woke up, regular time, had Cheerios—Mom won't let me have real cereal. Then I watched cartoons. Then Mom woke up, got a little mad that she slept so long, and we were going out to the car when—"

"Sweetheart," her mother interrupted, "just tell her what you saw."

Queen pointed with a short stiff arm at the sidewalk where her lunchbox still sat. "He fell right there by my lunchbox."

"Did he trip?"

"Oh, yes, ma'am, he didn't do it on purpose."

Neither woman could stifle their laughter.

"Well. You were *very* brave to run and get your mother. *Very* well done, Lara."

"Queen."

"Very well done, Queen." The officer bent down again to Queen's level. "Have you ever had a ride in a police car?"

"No, ma'am! Just ambulances. But those aren't very fun."

"Alright then." The officer laughed awkwardly. "Would you like a ride to school in my police car?" Then she looked at Queen's mother. "You can come too, of course. I'll run you back here."

Queen looked up at her mother and asked with her wide blue eyes.

"Sure," Laura said, but Queen was already turning around to grab her lunchbox.

Mother and daughter climbed into the back seat of the police cruiser and began their exciting journey to school just two miles away. Queen asked the officer a dozen questions about the car, the metal screen that kept the giddy little girl from climbing in the front seat, the siren and why they couldn't turn it on, the radio, her hat, the lights and why they couldn't turn them on either.

Then Queen asked one final question as they turned into the parking lot of her elementary school.

"Mom, can we give the man with the broken leg our Christmas Jar?"

I know I will feel so glad when I give the jar.
It won't be one million dollars, but it's some money they can
use, and they can use it however they wish.
—Montana

FOUR

Clark Maxwell stood beside Hope, who was flat on her back in her black dress with a Bible on her chest and still looking very much like the subject of a funeral and not simply a mourner. He noticed her hair was shorter than last time he'd buzzed through town, but still silky and shiny and styled in a no-nonsense, no-time-for-primping sort of way. She wore just enough makeup to remind people she probably didn't need any. Her lipstick was so light and natural Clark couldn't be completely sure she was wearing any.

He put his ear next to Hope's mouth to make sure she was breathing. He lingered a little longer to appreciate her perfume and accidentally bumped her shoulder with his.

Hope's eyes flashed open. "Um, hello!" she snapped.

Clark stepped back, partly embarrassed, but more amused than anything.

"You scared me to death," Hope said, sitting up on the table and fluffing the back of her flattened hair.

"Obviously."

Hope slid from the table to her feet and straightened her dress. "How long were you watching me?"

"Long enough to make sure you weren't dead."

"What made you think—" She stopped herself and set down the Bible. "Whatever. You don't just hover over someone, dead *or* alive." She looked around the tent to see who else had been watching her nap. "It's rude."

Clark extended his arms and invited a hug. "My mistake. You're clearly alive and in good health. And, I might add, looking as beautiful as ever."

Hope took a deep breath and stepped quickly in and out of the hug. "It's good to see you, Clark." She backed away and picked up the Bible again. "How's your dad? Did he come?"

"No, but he's good. Health isn't the best, but he's cranking along."

"Good. Tell him I said hello." Hope moved to the chair she'd been sitting in earlier and folded it up.

Clark followed and folded up the other.

"You're late, obviously. Most everyone has gone. Your mother is home with the grandkids. Your cousins went to the gravesite quite a while ago."

"The twins?"

Hope nodded.

Clark took Hope's chair from her and rested both upright against the table. "That's alright. I was pretty sure I wouldn't make it in time. And I didn't really know Chuck as well as most in town did."

"How could you *not* know Chuck?" Hope wondered, thinking that Clark must have forgotten their first meeting at the diner.

He folded his arms across his chest. "I guess I never was a fried chicken kinda guy."

Hope's face said, *That's odd.* Then her mouth said the same thing.

Three men entered the tent from the main opening. "Oh, sorry. We didn't know anyone was still here."

"You're fine," Hope said and walked quickly toward them, grateful for the distraction. "We're done. You here to take this tent down?"

"Yes, ma'am."

"Thank you," she said. "It suited us perfectly."

She smiled politely and walked out into the cooling late-afternoon air.

Clark followed. "Hope," he called to her as she crossed the parking lot, heading to the back door of the diner. "I thought I'd hang out a bit and wait for the twins. Could I come in and get something to drink?"

Hope opened the door. "I imagine so."

They wove through the kitchen and into the dining room. Chuck's two sons, Joel and Mike, sat in a corner booth.

"Hi, guys," Hope said. "This is Clark Maxwell. Uncle JJ's son."

They stood and shook hands. "Of course. We've met once or twice," Joel offered.

"Sorry about your dad," Clark said.

"Thanks." Joel clapped Clark on the shoulder. "It's been a tough week."

Hope handed Clark a glass of ice water. "I'm going to check on the guys outside. You're on your own."

Joel and Mike sat again in their booth. Mike made notes on a notepad and Joel tried to see how many sugar packets he could stack before they toppled over.

Clark sat on a round red stool at the old-fashioned counter and spun around to face the heart of the diner. A Christmas tree was up by the cash register, decorated with lights and silver tinsel and what appeared to be laminated coupons. Even the twenty-five-cent vending machine full of plastic toy bubbles had been draped with tinsel. Hidden inside the bubbles were tiny rings with funny chickens instead of diamonds. They might have been the only things unadorned by Christmas in the entire diner.

On the floor by the register was an upside-down box top holding a dozen or more Mason jars. On the wall behind the register were large framed photos of Christmas Jars with handwritten labels under each one. Most indicated location and amount. Some jars were short and fat with lids, others were only half-full of coins but topped with bills. One looked like a plastic five-gallon water cooler full of pennies. Clark scanned some of the labels.

———·———

$142.83—Buffalo, NY
$374.40—WW Robinson Elementary School
$3,103.50—Alpha Delta Kappa, Hot Springs, VA
$29.55—Portland, OR
$1,100—West Point Junior High

———·———

Now that Clark had noticed them, he realized there were similar photos on every wall of the diner. He spun back around for his water and saw newspaper clippings displayed under the glass countertop. He'd seen them there before, but had never bothered to read them.

———·———

Christmas Jar Saves Home from Foreclosure
Christmas Jars Ministry Takes Flight
Virginia Middle School Raises $800.00 with Christmas Jar for Accident Victim
Local Cancer Patient Receives Multiple Christmas Jars
Small Change, Big Hearts
Christmas Jars and Hope
Diner Becomes Home to Annual Christmas Jars Project

Clark read them all. He'd learned of the tradition from his father and his family had practiced it, but not annually and not to the extent that his Uncle Adam and Aunt Lauren had. He had no idea it had become such a movement or that Hope was now a pseudo-celebrity.

Clark lingered an extra moment on a story that included a color photo of Hope: *Hope's Christmas Jars Mission: Two Years Later*. The piece ran in the *Daily Record* and told of the two-year anniversary of Hope's inaugural Christmas Jar experience. It was also the anniversary of her reunion with her birth mother, Marianne. The story was written by Hope's new editor, Aimee, and proudly reported how the Christmas Jar tradition had grown beyond the county and was finding traction across the state. Clark looked to the left and right and spotted even more clips neatly displayed one after another all the way to each end of the counter.

Before he could finish reading another article, Hope, the twins, and their husbands reappeared from the kitchen.

"Clark!" Clara and Julie burst through the swinging door and hugged him at the same time. He put his broad arms around their waists and lifted them both off the ground.

"Look what I found," Clark said. "Pip and Squeak." He kissed both of them on the cheek before gently setting them back on the floor. Tyson and Braden gave a quick wave and slid into the corner booth with friends Joel and Mike.

"You're here," Clara said. "So you're doing it? I hadn't heard."

"Not sure yet, but it seemed like the right time to come." He gestured for them to sit and they took stools on either side of him. "I'm sorry I missed the service today."

"No worries." Julie stole a sip of Clark's water. "We're just glad you're here. How long are you staying?"

"Until I decide about the shop, I guess."

"Hope, did you know Clark was thinking of taking over the business?" Clara asked.

"I'd heard." Hope took a clean rag and began wiping down counters that didn't need wiping down.

"I just don't think Hannah and Dustin are happy doing this anymore," Clara continued in a half-whisper. "And Dad would *want* them to be happy. It's so much harder than they thought it would be. I don't think any of us realized how much work the shop was and how much of it Dad was doing alone. I can hardly stand to go in there anymore because it just doesn't feel like Restored anymore."

"It's different," Julie added.

"Sure is," Clara agreed.

Clark finished his water and began crunching a piece of ice. "Who knows what the future holds, but I promised Aunt Lauren I'd spend some time here during the off-season and think it over. It's a huge step moving here, but I loved your dad and maybe I'm ready for a change."

"What about that big baseball career?" Hope asked.

"My heart's still in the batter's box, but my swing isn't. We'll see . . . maybe I can make it work here." Clark slipped another ice cube in his mouth and began chewing it.

Hope abruptly stopped wiping down the counters and carried the rag back into the kitchen.

Clark waited to see if she'd return. When she didn't, he stepped around to the other side of the counter and leaned over to whisper at both girls. "What's *her* deal?"

"Deal?" Julie said.

"I've never seen her like this. She's spun tighter than a kite spool."

"She's just stressed," Clara said. "You know how she gets. And you didn't exactly leave on great terms last time." She punched him in the arm.

"Have you ever left on good terms?" Julie added.

"Of course," he said. "Chuck's Labor Day picnic." He smiled, already lost in the memory of a water balloon fight gone terribly wrong.

Clara looked at Julie. "No comment, right, Jules?"

"Right-o. Hope's like a sister now," Julie said. "More than ever. We love her, Clark. Mom loves her, too. And Dad thought the *world* of her. Hope misses him almost as much as we do. Especially during jar time."

"She's just focused right now," Julie added. "That's all. If she seems cold it's just because she's buried in Christmas Jars."

"It's taken off?" Clark asked.

"Uh-huh," Julie nodded. "Like no one ever predicted. Way

bigger than last year even. People all over give jars now and Chuck's has become the center of it—the hub. It's not a formal organization or anything like that, but it's become almost a Christmas Jars Ministry here. Some even call it that. Hope and Marianne run everything from here. Hope's been on the news, in magazines. It's a movement now."

"And your dad started it all," Clark said. "You must be proud."

"We sure are," Clara spoke up and Clark remembered how in sync the twins had always been. "After Dad died Chuck totally picked up the idea and ran with it. Chuck was a big believer in the jars. He probably gave away as many as Dad did in just a couple years."

"How's Hope's day job?" Clark asked.

"Going great. Hope's column was picked up this fall by some other papers. She's syndicated now—probably in a dozen or so small papers, right Jules?"

Julie nodded. "Uh-huh. It's a big break. She changed the name, too. It's called 'Hopeful Words' now. She's getting *really* good."

Hope swung back through the door.

"Quit fussing, Hope, and come sit down," Julie said.

"Maybe later. I'm having dinner with Marianne and Nick. They've got some big announcement."

"Any idea what's up?" Julie asked.

"Not a clue. With those two, who knows. Could be anything. I'll see you all soon though." She gave the twins each a hug and went to say good-bye to the four men in the far corner of the diner. She patted Joel on the shoulder. "If there's anything I can do, call me, OK? Your dad would be so proud of his boys." She hugged them all good-bye and walked back toward the kitchen door.

As she neared Clark he stood and extended his arm to block her path. "Gotta pay the toll. Don't I get another hug, too?"

She smiled sarcastically. "You can't afford another one."

"Ooooh," the twins cackled in unison.

"Come on, let's start fresh."

"Riiight. We can start fresh when you buy me new shoes and apologize for dumping me in the river in front of my boss at the picnic." She lifted his arm and passed underneath and out the door.

Clark wasn't smiling, but Hope sure was.

"She'll get over it," Clara said.

"Yeah, she'll warm up," Julie nodded.

"To what?" Clark asked. "Freezing?"

I saved all year and am so blessed to be able to do this.
Will I do it again? Without a doubt.
This has allowed me to reopen my heart.
—Kathy

FIVE

In his hospital bed, Al crunched ice from a Dixie cup and stared across the room at the tiny television suspended from the ceiling. The dino-era television remote had an unpredictable demeanor he could relate to. It only worked about half the time; at the moment, it wasn't.

Al's nurse had become gradually grouchier as the afternoon became evening and the last thing he wanted—besides another date with the bedpan—was to see Nurse Jessica again. Unable to change the channel since her last visit to his third floor room, Al had been watching an infomercial for a groundbreaking men's girdle that promised better fitting slacks and shorts. He was quickly running out of ice . . . and patience.

"Listen guys, *trust* me"—the announcer had a fake British accent that sometimes slipped into Australian—"your pants will feel like they were *custom-made* for your waist. Your shirts will *drape* differently, you'll have the *flat stomach* you always wanted but couldn't achieve even with *sit-ups, crunches,* or those *disgusting* diets. Plus, the patent-pending Flab Strap doesn't just *pull* in the flab and *seal* your tummy in place, it also *burns* fat by raising your core body temperature with our revolutionary heat strips sewn right into the fabric."

If it didn't end soon, Al was prepared to throw things at the tiny power button on the front of the television until it either powered off or the set fell to the floor and shattered.

He turned away from the TV and noticed a nurse passing down the hallway holding hands with a young girl in a hospital gown who looked remarkably like his sidewalk heroine.

Suddenly the Australian-Brit's voice rose to a near shout. "Men, call *right now.* Don't wait another *second.* And *women,* yes, *women,* you too, pick one up for your sweetheart who's let himself go. Call in the next *ten minutes* for your Flab Strap and I'll throw in a *second* Flab Strap, *and* I'll ship it for free, *and . . .*" The pitchman's voice rose as he stretched his hands out toward the camera with his index fingers extended and pointed at his eager viewers.

"Wait for it . . ." Al said to the television.

"There's more!"

Al pushed the nurses' button. "Nurse? *Please,* any nurse."

A moment later Nurse Jessica appeared in the doorway. "Everything OK?"

"Could you change the channel for me? Anything but this."

She stood next to the television and quickly flipped through the hospital's eleven channels. "See anything you like?" She didn't work very hard to mask her impatience.

"One more time. Wait! What was that on channel thirteen?"

She pushed the up arrow until the channel indicator read "13" and on screen a middle-aged man with a goatee was sitting beside a pool being interviewed. A graphic at the bottom read "Matt B., Farmington, Utah."

"I don't want to exaggerate," the man said thoughtfully, "but the Flab Strap has changed my life."

"Off!" Al blurted. "Just turn it off."

Nurse Jessica hid a grin, but not very well, Al noticed. "You could sleep," she said. "It's after midnight." She checked his IV and pushed a few buttons on the monitor. "How's the pain?"

"Painful," he said.

"I can't give you more medication without checking with Dr. Garman, and he won't be back until morning."

"Fine," he mumbled.

"Try to sleep, Mr. Allred. It's been a long day." Then she mumbled under her breath, "Mostly for me."

He turned his head to watch her walk out. He'd decided the first time she came in that she was cute, but she was probably twenty-five years younger than he was, so there wasn't much use being nice.

"Nurse," he called. "You ever tried to sleep with pins in your legs?"

"Can't say that I have, no."

"Come back and give me advice when you have."

She forced a polite smile and began to leave the room, but before the door was completely shut behind her, she pulled it back open, returned to the television, and flipped it back on.

Her next smile wasn't forced at all.

I received a Christmas Jar.
It brought tears to my eyes and gave me goose bumps.
It's such a beautiful secret.
—Karen

SIX

6:45 AM. Hope awoke in the same apartment she'd shared with her mother during college. The same apartment she'd returned to one Christmas Eve to find it broken into and ransacked. But most important for Hope, it was the same apartment where she'd discovered the tradition of the Christmas Jar, and, eventually, been reunited with her birth mother, Marianne.

No one could deny the tradition and rapidly spreading movement hadn't just changed Hope's life, it had changed Hope. Once driven to win a Pulitzer for breaking the story-of-the-century and later to run the newsroom at the *Washington Post* or *New York Times,* she now spent her days expanding the Christmas Jars tradition and writing her syndicated column, "Hopeful Words."

The columnist gig began with her original Christmas Jars

front-page story, the piece responsible for bringing Marianne back into her life and laying the first stones on her path to forgiveness with the Maxwell family. Reader reaction was so passionate that her editor asked for three additional columns on the tradition and her reunion with Marianne. The articles also included anecdotes from other real-life jar givers and recipients. Not only had Hope met her goal of putting herself on the map, but she'd also made famous the *Daily Record,* Chuck's Chicken 'n' Biscuits, and the tradition itself.

Hope rolled over in bed, slid her arms under her pillow, stared up at the ceiling, and replayed dinner the night before with Marianne and Nick.

After leaving the funeral and the diner, Hope had hurried to Marianne and Nick's home for dinner and a quiet evening after three hectic, frantic days. Their home was just three blocks south of Main Street and a short walk to Marianne's salon. Hope was grateful to have them so close. Their cozy Cape Cod cottage offered an escape from life, from Chuck's, from writing deadlines, and from bad dates.

Hope and Marianne had slipped into a comfortable relationship. It wasn't the same as she'd enjoyed with Louise—the woman who'd raised her—but it was sweet and tender in different ways. And though Hope still missed the woman who discovered her at Chuck's and raised her as her own, she thanked God everyday that he'd delivered Marianne back into her life.

Marianne's much-hyped "exciting announcement" was just that. After thirteen Christmases together, and two more working alongside Hope and the gang at Chuck's in the Christmas Jars Ministry, Marianne's dream was coming true.

"Hope," Marianne began after they'd finished loading the dishwasher together and joined Nick in the living room. "We've got some news, some exciting, wonderful, never-thought-it-would-really-happen news."

Nick took her hand.

"This has been a dream of mine for so long," she continued, "but when you experience what I have—the trials, the heartbreak, the loneliness of being single for so long before Nick came along . . . Well, I guess you give up on things like this."

Nick winked at Hope.

"When Nick and I were dating I told him this was a goal of mine, something I wanted—no—*needed* to do and I wasn't getting any younger. I made him promise we'd do this. Because you know the older you get the harder it is to—"

"Heavens, Marianne," Hope sprang from the couch. "Are you pregnant?"

Marianne looked at Nick, confused.

Nick looked at Hope, confused *and* terrified.

Hope asked again, "Well are you?"

Marianne and Nick fell into laughter and in Marianne's case, uncontrollable giggles, which were likely heard on Main Street.

"Sweetheart," Marianne said, wiping tears from her eyes, "what in the world gave you *that* idea?"

Hope, still standing, put her hands on her hips. "Blah blah, the older you get the harder it is to—"

"Travel." Marianne finished her sentence and began laughing again.

Hope fell back into the comfortable cushions of the leather couch.

"Hope, Marianne is fifty years old." Nick tried not to laugh, but it was hard with Marianne's head buried in a throw pillow on his lap and her entire body shaking.

"OK, OK," Hope said, "I get it. Ha-ha, joke's on Hope." Even she couldn't help but smile.

Marianne sat up and fussed with her hair. "Oh, my, *that's* one for the journal."

"How did we miss that coming?" Nick said and tenderly wiped a stray eyelash from his wife's cheek.

"Oh, my," Marianne said again as she reached into her purse on the floor by the couch. She pulled out a handful of brochures and set them down on the coffee table between them. "We're taking a trip."

"*That's* the big announcement?"

"Not just any trip, dear, a *vacation*. And we wanted you to be supportive." Marianne looked at Nick. "Right?"

"Of course," he said, nodding.

"That's wonderful. Why in heaven's name wouldn't I be supportive?"

"It's a long trip," Marianne said.

"Terrific."

"Three weeks," Nick said.

"Fantastic, where are you going?"

"Pretty far," Marianne said.

Nick nodded again. "That's an understatement."

"This is so exciting! When do you leave?"

Marianne and Nick looked at one another.

"We leave in two days," Marianne said as she slid the brochures across the coffee table to Hope.

She picked them up. "Jerusalem?" Her mouth hung open.

"All of it. The Garden Tomb, Bethlehem, Galilee, Jordan, Mount Sinai."

Hope stood and stepped over the table to hug Marianne. "This is your official honeymoon, isn't it? You're *finally* getting it! I am so, so, so happy you're doing this." Hope tugged on Nick and lassoed him into the hug.

"Wait." Hope stepped back. "You're not nervous about traveling there? Isn't it dangerous?"

"Not as much as you'd think, dear. And that's partly why we're doing a group trip—there'll be about fifty of us total. Strength in numbers and very good security."

"I guess that'd be true," Hope reluctantly agreed.

"Just one more thing, Hope," Marianne said. "We're also going to Cairo, to see the Pyramids, the Valley of the Kings, the Luxor Temple—"

"The whole shebang," Nick interrupted.

"How long did you say you'd be gone?" Hope asked.

Nick and Marianne sat again and pulled Hope down on the

couch between them. "That's the thing, sweetheart, it's a three-week trip because there's so much ground to cover."

Once again Hope did math in her head. "Oh."

"Is that alright? I never thought it would work out this way, I really didn't, but we're saving money by going on a tour with other couples, and it's a special December trip. We'll wake up Christmas morning in Bethlehem. Imagine that!"

Hope did. And though she'd miss them both and their annual dinner at Chuck's, she knew Marianne deserved nothing less.

"I think it's the sweetest thing ever." Hope kissed Nick on the cheek. "You're a good man."

"You'll be OK with the project this year?" Marianne patted Hope's hand. "Because honestly, Hope, that's what made this so hard. Not being here to help you with the jars. I told Nick probably a hundred different times we should cancel. Especially with Chuck's passing. It's a lot to leave you with."

"Now stop. Don't you dare. We'll be fine. Gayle needs to be busy right now anyway. So she'll carry a little extra load. Plus with Lauren, Eva, Hannah, the twins—we'll get it done."

All three stood up and Marianne again pulled Hope into a tight embrace. But this time she didn't let go before speaking. "I love you, Hope Jensen. You're such a good girl. Louise would be so proud of you this year."

"You think?"

"*I know,*" Marianne said. "Thank you for being happy for

us. Now you give those jars away, you change some lives, and then you write all about it just like we planned."

"I will," Hope said, still wrapped up in Marianne's arms.

"Nick says we'll have Internet access at most of the places we're staying, maybe all of them, so I'll be watching for your columns." She finally released her and put her hands on her face. "You can do it."

"Thanks." She looked into Marianne's eyes. "I'll break the record, trust me. I'll give away more jars than ever. I'll do it for Adam, for Chuck, for you. I promise."

"Just remember," Marianne said with just the slightest hint of authority. "It's not about an army of jars. It's about *one. One* jar. *One* birth. *One* Savior."

I feel so blessed. God has given me so much and I just can't imagine why He allowed me to be blessed even more with this Christmas Jar. I am very humbled.
—Kimberly

SEVEN

M r. Allred?"

Al heard the voice, but was convinced it was the public address announcer in his dream where he'd just won the gold medal in ironing-board surfing on the North Shore.

"Mr. Allred? It's Dr. Garman."

Al opened his eyes just enough to see the too-young and too-slender doctor standing over him. He didn't know what blinded him more: the lights above, the doctor's cleanly pressed smock, or the doctor's perfectly white teeth.

"Welcome back," Dr. Garman said. "You slept well."

"I did?"

"You sure did. Night shift said you had a difficult time dozing off, so a colleague approved something a bit stronger for sleep."

"A bit?"

Dr. Garman smiled. "You slept for fourteen hours."

"So why do I feel worse than I did right after the surgery?"

"That will fade. We've still got heavy meds in your drip." Dr. Garman flipped open Al's chart and made some notes. "How's the leg?"

"I feel like the Ten-Million-Dollar Man."

The doctor met Al's sarcasm with the same "Whatever" reaction he'd flashed when he'd first been introduced to Al's sense of humor twenty-four hours earlier. "Let's take a look." He pulled the blanket back and checked the bandages. "Oh, very well done. You stayed nice and dry through the night. Good job."

"Gee thanks, kiddo."

"Touché." He gave a thumbs-up. "So here's the plan of attack, Mr. Allred. We're going to keep you another day. Surgery went well, took longer than expected, but the result was positive. Sometime tomorrow we'll put the leg in a cast and get you home. I thought we'd need to go all the way to the hip, but the damage was confined below the knee. You're going to be sore, the knee especially, but you'll get a calf-and-ankle cast only." He started writing on the chart again. "Take it easy, as easy as life will allow, and come back in a few weeks."

"Why?"

"X-rays. We've got to be sure the pins don't move around on us."

Dr. Garman covered Al's leg again and adjusted his IV. "It

doesn't sound or feel like it today, but you'll be fine. Your break was serious and there was a lot of bone to piece back together, but I've seen worse. You'll make it. Be patient, take your time to heal, and you'll be back to normal in no time."

"What about working?"

"You can work in a couple days, if you feel up to it, but you'll still need to keep the leg elevated as much as possible. Maybe a pillow on the chair next to you, something like that."

"Driving?"

"In this cast? No. I'm afraid you won't be driving for a month—you *shouldn't* be that is, but I can't baby-sit you. Play it by ear depending on how fast you heal."

"Terrific." Already Al was wondering how long it would take for Cowboy Craig to pick up the keys to the van and warehouse.

"But there's good news," Dr. Garman said. "You've got visitors. They've been in the lobby for two hours waiting for you to wake up."

"Visitors?"

"Yes, I'll send them down." He pulled open the door, but Al's voice stopped him.

"Is one of them wearing a cowboy hat?"

Dr. Garman shook his head and left.

Moments later the little girl and her mother opened the door. The girl carried a shoebox with both hands. Her mother carried a plate of pecan brownies.

"Hi, Mr. Allred," the girl said. "How are you?" She began

to sit on the side of his bed, but her mother tugged on the back of her pants. "No, no, dear, we can stand. We have to be very, very careful around Mr. Allred. He's in a lot of pain."

The girl set the heavy shoebox on the bed instead. "Does your leg still hurt?"

"Oh, yes," he stammered. He put his hands at his sides and pushed himself up to a half-sitting position for the first time since tumbling down the stairs and snapping his leg into several pieces.

The girl leaned in and probably meant to whisper, but it came out only slightly softer than her typical too-loud speaking voice. "My name is Lara Ross, or Queen Lara, or just Queen if you like, and this is my mother, Laura, but with a U, in case you forgot."

"He didn't forget," Laura said.

"Of course not," Al answered. "You don't forget names like that." Al didn't recall ever actually knowing their names, but he was sure he wouldn't forget them now. He reached for his water but quickly realized Dr. Garman had moved the tray back when he accessed the IV stand.

"Here, let me," Laura said and she handed him the cup.

"Thanks," he said and took a long drink, capturing an ice cube with his teeth before stretching again to reach the tray he knew was still out of reach.

"I got it," Laura offered.

"Thanks."

As Al pushed himself up a few more inches, the door

cracked open and an unfamiliar nurse poked her head in. "Hi, Queen. I thought that was you I saw downstairs."

"Hi, Nurse James!" Queen ran and hugged her in the doorway.

Nurse James bent down and whispered something in Queen's ear.

Queen covered her mouth and giggled. "Yes, ma'am. See you tomorrow."

The nurse waved good-bye to Queen's mother and let the door shut behind her.

"We don't want to keep you, but we brought you some brownies. We thought you might enjoy something from outside the hospital." Laura set the plastic-wrap-covered paper plate on his tray and slid it within reach.

"They're the very best brownies Mom makes," Queen chimed proudly. "Mom likes chocolate and she makes a lot of brownies—pecan, caramel, walnut—"

"Alright, sweetheart, why don't you show him what's in the shoebox."

Queen started to take the lid off, hesitated, and returned it to its place. "We haven't even found out how he's doing yet."

Laura folded her arms. "It's not polite to pry, Queen—"

"It's no problem." Even Al was a little surprised the words came out. "If not for you two, I might still be lying on the sidewalk."

"*I* was the one who spotted you," Queen said.

Al's eyes smiled. "Yes, you did."

"So is your leg better now?"

"Not better, but fixed. They put pins in my leg to hold all the bones together."

Queen raised her hand. "Mommy puts pins in my church dress sometimes."

"His pins are a little different, Queen." Laura walked around to Queen's side of the bed and put her hands on her shoulders. "Why don't you show him what you brought."

Queen removed the shoebox lid and pulled out a glass jar full of coins. It had a lid on it, but someone had tied it shut anyway with green yarn. It also had a black-and-gold label across the side that read *Christmas Jar.*

She held it out for Al.

"What's this?" He took the jar and looked up at Laura.

"It's our Christmas Jar," Queen answered instead. "We've been saving change all year for you."

"Not knowing it was for you, of course," her mother said. "It's a tradition we've done for a few years—ever since we got our first jar—and normally we would give it away anonymously, but Queen insisted we hand it to you personally."

Queen's face lit up.

"She can be persistent," her mother added.

"I bet," Al said. He twisted the jar around, marveling at how heavy a few dollars in change could be.

"That's nice, but I can't take it." He set the jar back down in the shoebox.

"Why not?" Queen asked.

"I barely know you."

"So?" Queen's voice rose.

"It's not about that, Mr. Allred," Laura said. "It's about a small token. It's not a lot of money, as you can see, but we're passing along the tradition the way someone passed it along to Queen and me. That's how it works."

"I'm flattered you thought of me, and it was nice of you to come visit, and I will keep the delicious brownies, but give the jar to someone who needs it more."

"I think *you* need it," Queen pressed and her blue eyes narrowed.

"Lara Q! That's enough now. Let's leave Mr. Allred to rest."

Queen put the lid on the box, lifted it up, and cradled it in her arms.

Al slid back down and rested his head on his pillow.

"Is there anything else we can get you?" Laura asked.

"No, thanks."

"Good-bye then," Laura said. "Hope to see you around the complex soon."

He nodded and looked at Queen, but she simply turned around, the shoebox still clutched tightly against her chest, and walked out the door her mother held open.

When the two were both in the hallway and the door had finally drifted shut, Al watched through the window blinds as Laura bent down and said something to her downtrodden daughter.

Queen said something back and smiled.

Then they hugged for a minute or two before Laura took Queen's hand and they disappeared around the corner.

Al ate a brownie, then another, drank a cup and a half of water, and dozed off to sleep again. When he awoke there was a familiar looking Christmas Jar on his bedside tray with a blue hospital sticky note on the side.

———————

Mr. Allred, Queen always wins. ☺ *The miracle starts with you.*

I was given a gift of hope tonight, a Christmas Jar.
It said, "It doesn't matter where things come from,
what matters is that someone CARES."
—Robin

EIGHT

H ope spent a quiet morning in her apartment. She hadn't realized how long it had been since she had nowhere to be, no one to comfort, no meals to plan, funerals to attend, or deadlines to meet.

She took a long shower, so long, in fact, that she ran out of hot water, something she'd rarely done since the days of sharing a hot-water heater with her departed mother, Louise.

Hope dressed, towel dried and combed her hair, fixed a bowl of oatmeal and ate it sitting on the futon with her feet propped up. Her toes needed polishing, she noticed, and she made a mental note to get them done before Christmas at Tres' Bella, a new and swanky salon northwest of town. But she examined her feet more closely and, fearing the thought would be lost like so many others, she picked up the phone and called for an appointment.

There were dishes in the sink, Hope remembered, some

almost a week old. *My mother would ground me if she were alive,* she thought. She did them quickly.

The scrapbooks Louise left behind hadn't been cracked open since summer. Hope pulled one from the shelf and savored the memories. Photos of Louise in front of a home they often cleaned together when Louise still had her cleaning company. A photo of Hope sitting in a booth at Chuck's Chicken 'n' Biscuits celebrating her Sweet Sixteenth, with her arm around Chuck's wife, Gayle. Another photo from the same day—Hope sitting behind the wheel of one of Chuck's prized Mustangs. He'd let her drive it up a few miles and back down U.S. Highway 4. She suddenly felt blue recalling how she'd turned around that day in the very cemetery that Chuck now rested in.

The phone startled her.

"Hello?"

"Hope Jensen?" a voice said.

Hope heard music in the background and instantly put her hand against her forehead. "I am so sorry. Is this 102.5?"

"Yep, and don't sweat it," DJ Blake said in a voice that didn't sound anything like he would in a few seconds on the radio. "You're a busy lady, I hear. Still a go for this morning?"

"Yes, and again, I'm sorry. I'm never late for these things."

"No sweat. Hang tight. Back to you and live in two."

Hope ran for her planner in her bedroom to make sure she hadn't missed anything else that morning. Then she walked to the bathroom with the cordless phone pressed against her ear. She checked her hair and smiled at her own vanity.

A moment later she heard DJ Blake welcoming her to the air. "We are so excited this morning to be joined by a woman whose mission is to make Christmas something you think about every day of the year. Her name is Hope Jensen and she's a busy lady, folks, so we're lucky to get a few minutes of her time. Hope, welcome to the Blake Show."

"Thanks for having me, Blake. Love your show."

"And thank you, Hope, for that, and for giving us time this morning. So tell us, what is a Christmas Jar and why should it matter? I keep hearing about these things from my listeners and where better to get the straight scoop than from the inventor herself."

"Oh, no, I'm not the inventor, Blake. I'm just someone trying to take the Christmas Jars message mainstream. I might have been one of the first to get one and later on to *give* one, but the tradition predates me."

"Alright then, so just what *is* a Christmas Jar?"

"Easy. A Christmas Jar is an empty pickle jar, or mayonnaise jar, or whatever, that you wash out and place on your counter. Then every day, without fail, you drop in your spare change. Mom goes to the store and comes home with change, it goes in the jar. Dad buys a soda at the convenience store, the change goes in the jar. Kids buy ice cream for lunch at school, they run home and first things first, the change goes in the jar. Then on or around Christmas Eve you give the jar away anonymously to someone in need. Some need money, some need love, some need hope."

"How refreshing in this world, right?"

"Definitely. And I've heard hundreds of stories about jars being given away, but I want your listeners to know it doesn't matter how much money is in the jar. Always remember that the bigger message is that you're aware of someone's needs."

"Great advice, Hope. If you're just joining us, friends, we're talking to Hope Jensen, a Christmas Jars pioneer and the woman who's almost single-handedly taking the Christmas Jars magic from a small-town tradition to mainstream prominence."

Hope smiled.

"Now my producer tells me you're doing something slightly different this year. Something more coordinated than in years past. Tell us about it, and specifically how we can get involved."

"That's right, Blake, the tradition has been gaining steam for a number of years, but we thought this year we'd shoot even bigger and organize our efforts more to really capture and distribute as many Christmas Jars as possible."

"Sounds challenging, go on."

"You may not have heard of it, but we're blessed with an old-school chicken place up here called Chuck's Chicken 'n' Biscuits. It's a diner on Highway 4 halfway between not much and nowhere."

The host laughed. "We can relate, trust me! But I have to tell you, Hope, I've been to Chuck's before while passing through and it's a wonderful slice of Americana. In fact, that's where I first heard of the Christmas Jars. The place is practically a poultry theme park as well as a monument to the Christmas Jars movement."

"So true." Hope returned the laughter but quickly trailed off to a more somber tone. "The bad news, and this was a real personal loss for me, is that our community lost Chuck last week on Thanksgiving night."

Blake let the moment settle.

"Now that you mention it, I'd heard that. I'm very sorry. Sounds like you were close. My condolences."

"Much appreciated. He was a good man."

"I bet he was." Blake hesitated again. "Unfortunately we're running up against a hard newsbreak. Real quick, tell us about your plans for the Christmas Jar project this year."

Hope had already given so many interviews since the early part of November that her answer was practically memorized word-for-word.

"We understand that not everyone is comfortable giving a jar away on a doorstep or street corner. That's OK. This year we're inviting you to drop off your jar at the diner—"

"Chuck's Chicken 'n' Biscuits."

"That's right. And we'll deliver your jar for you to families or individuals in need. Our goal this year is a thousand and one jars. Last year we collected and distributed a hundred and one. Drop yours off or send it in, and we'll give you a new jar—free, of course—to begin filling for next year. Easy as Chuck's Three Musketeers pie."

"A thousand and one? Wow! I bet our listeners are curious, why so many? Is there significance to the number?"

"Excellent question. On Christmas Eve last year, someone came into the diner—"

"Chuck's Chicken 'n' Biscuits."

"Right. And this man had a jar to contribute to the cause but didn't know who to give it to or how. He needed our help. As we stood there chatting, we watched a young family of five pile out of a ragged and rusty van and into Chuck's. They sat and ordered two meals to share among them, not a bit of complaining either. It really touched us both, and though I don't remember his name, I remember he walked right over to this little family and gave them his jar. Then he walked back over to me and said, 'If this is how much good a single jar can do, imagine what *a thousand* jars could do.'"

"And here we are today. With one really big goal and only a few weeks to get there."

Hope could hear Blake smiling through the phone. "I love it," he said. "What a great idea. Where can 102.5 listeners go for more information?"

"Come by the diner anytime, it's the source of all things Christmas Jars, or visit us at Chuck's web site, designed by Chuck himself, at www.ChucksChickenAndBiscuits.com." She repeated the web address, then Blake did, too, just to be sure.

"Thank you again, Hope, you're a real inspiration. Come back after Christmas and let us know how you did. God bless. And now the news."

The line crackled and popped and Hope hung up the phone. *There aren't many things I enjoy more than that,* she thought, *except TV interviews.*

I've often wondered how a person repays kindness.
I know now . . . with a Christmas Jar. As if a year full
of blessings wasn't already enough, God blessed me again
tonight. And tomorrow? A new jar begins.
—Patricia

NINE

A l lay on his couch with his left leg propped up on three pillows. His leg still hurt enough to gripe about, but his armpits hurt even more from the crutches.

Cowboy Craig was happy to drive him home that morning from the hospital, but his motives were mixed. On the one hand, he said, he was terribly sorry for Al's troubles and wished him a speedy recovery. But he also needed to tell him face-to-face that he was being let go.

"I just can't afford to keep you, Al. I'm sorry. Sales are down, costs are up, and now you're unable to drive for a while."

"It's my left leg," Al offered. "I can drive as soon as I'm off the pills."

"Maybe so, but we've been thinking of combining yours and Scrubb's areas anyway." He looked down at his cowboy boots. "You've been in Idaho Falls for a while, and let's be honest, you're always complaining. So maybe a change would do you good. You know, a fresh start. Maybe earn some real money somewhere. Al, this might be a blessing in disguise."

"For who?"

Cowboy Craig apologized again and assured Al his health insurance would be good for another month. They shook hands a final time and he handed Al an envelope. "I wish it were more," he said and showed himself out the door.

Al opened the envelope and found a full month's pay. He wanted to be angry, but even he recognized it was much more than his former boss needed to do for him.

He picked up a stack of drawings he'd found under the door when he arrived home that morning. Flowers. Waterfalls. Little girls wearing pink dresses and crowns. He actually grinned at one drawing depicting a stick figure child with giant muscles carrying a man with only one and a half legs.

He looked at the pile of belongings Cowboy Craig had helped him cart home from the hospital. A pill bottle and a prescription for more. A folder full of insurance paperwork he'd probably never read. His Christmas Jar. He bent down and picked up the heavy jar, admiring it once more. Al had never done something quite so noble as fill a jar for a stranger, but he reminded himself he hadn't always been so jaded. He'd donated money for causes before, even been to a corporate service project or two through the years. Bought Girl Scout cookies. Put money in the offering plate at church, though he didn't remember ever doing that without a woman sitting beside him looking very impressed.

Al saw a crumpled bill at the very bottom of the jar and held it up to see if he could tell the denomination without dumping the change out. *A twenty,* he thought. *Not bad.* He also noticed a sticky label on the bottom.

Someone loves you!
You're holding a Christmas Jar!
The miracle starts with you!
www.ChucksChickenAndBiscuits.com

He set the jar down and stretched to reach under the couch. He felt his laptop, hidden right where he had left it on his way to work the day his leg played toothpick. The battery was nearly dead, but he fired it up anyway and punched in the address. A clean and organized, but obviously homemade, web site slowly loaded. Al wondered if it was finally time for faster service. He also wondered who had designed the amateurish web site.

A Christmas Jars banner caught his eye: *Got Jars?* He clicked on it and was taken to a page with the words *Christmas Jars Ministry* splashed atop the menu bar.

---

min-is-try: a person or thing through which something is accomplished; ministration; service.
We are not preachers or pastors, but we preach charity.

*We are not a legally organized entity, but we are organized.
We are here for you!*

The page featured ideas for collecting change, tips on giving jars away, and stories of people claiming to be miraculously affected by jars both given or received. In the left menu bar was a picture of an average-looking man and a very attractive woman. *He sure married up,* Al thought.

The caption below the photo read *Chuck and Gayle Quillon: In love to the end.* Further below were the words *In Memory of Chuck* and a link to his obituary in what appeared to be the web site for a local paper.

Al drilled deeper into the site and found a photo library. He clicked one by one through pictures of children holding jars, jars on counters, a toddler putting a quarter in a jar, jars that were carefully painted, glass jars, plastic jars, jars on a table in a restaurant, another attractive woman standing at a lunch counter in front of a long row of jars—thirty or more—each filled to the brim with money.

"This is really something," Al mumbled to the screen.

He lingered on another photo of Chuck's widow, Gayle, holding a stuffed chicken and standing next to a boy named Andrew in a wheelchair. He held a huge Christmas Jar in his lap and wore the broadest smile. So did she.

On another page he found a paragraph about the restaurant's goal of collecting 1,001 jars to redistribute that year on

Christmas Eve and a counter showing how many they'd collected as of December third. Only 269.

"They'll never make it without more exposure," he scoffed.

There was also a plea on the site for volunteers to help coordinate activities from the diner.

He spotted a link to a collection of media appearances by a woman named Hope Jensen, the same woman pictured standing proudly at the lunch counter with an array of jars. She'd been on several morning TV shows and radio programs, though none he'd ever heard of. The articulate young woman was on a mission, she said in every interview, to spread the tradition to every kitchen counter in the world.

He briefly touched the jar on the floor and then covered himself up with the blanket Cowboy Craig had retrieved from the bedroom. He closed his eyes and considered his new reality.

No job. No leads. No woman to cook for him. No end to the stack of credit card bills that reflected his long-honed gift of spending more than he made. No reason to stay in Idaho Falls.

He wondered how big the Christmas Jars tradition could become if it had the right person pushing from behind. *Maybe I'm the one who could put a jar on every counter in America,* he thought. *Could this be more than just goodwill, could it also be profitable goodwill?*

Eventually he drifted into the peaceful space between worry and sleep and dreamed of pretty widows, Mason jars, and fried chicken.

The next morning he wrote checks for his rent and utilities

and mailed them all a few days early. Then he stumbled on his crutches to Queen and Laura's apartment, thanked them for the drawings, returned the Christmas Jar in a shopping bag he'd slung over his shoulder, and asked for a ride to the train station.

It was awkward for everyone, but he even let Queen hug him when they said good-bye at the ticket counter.

"Where are you going?" she asked.

"Just on a short trip for the holidays."

"Are you coming back?"

"I hope so."

"But we just became friends."

Queen's mother watched from a short distance.

Al's comfort zone was rapidly shrinking.

"I know. I'll be back. I just need a break. Adults need breaks sometimes."

Queen whispered, "That's what Mom says when she watches Oprah."

Laura stepped closer. "What was that?"

Queen grinned at Al.

Laura wagged her finger playfully at her daughter. "Mr. Allred," she said, "is your leg well enough for this? It's only been a few days."

"Well enough." He paused. "Pain pills and crutches—I'm good."

Queen motioned for Al to bend down again. "Why did you give back our Christmas Jar?"

Al looked up at Laura. "I just thought there might be

someone who needs it more. My leg's broken, that's all. I'm not suffering."

"Mom says some people don't *like* to be helped, even when they need it," Queen said.

It wasn't clear who Queen had embarrassed more, Al or her mother, but both shifted uncomfortably as their eyes seemed to suddenly find something interesting in the distance.

Laura broke the silence. "Queen, would you mind waiting in the car, darling? It's just right there. I can see you."

Queen agreed and hugged Al a final time. "Bye, my new friend." She looked through him. "Get better." Both Laura and Al watched as she looked both ways four or five times before scurrying across the parking lot to the car.

"Mr. Allred—"

"Al."

"Al," she said and her eyes brightened. "Queen is different. She latches on to people, you probably noticed."

"Ya think?" He didn't intend for it to sound so sarcastic.

"She worries about other people. A lot. It takes her mind off her own problems."

Al glanced at his watch. "What problems does Queen have? Other than being a talker and asking more questions than most of us have answers."

"She's dying." Laura uttered the words softly, but they still rang through the train station platform.

"Dying?"

"Her heart. She was born with congenital heart disease and even as she's grown, her heart has deteriorated. She's been on the transplant list for a long time, but it should go without saying . . . it's an uphill battle. . . . Such hard odds . . . but you probably know this."

"Not really," he mumbled. Al had struggled through divorce, legal battles, broken relationships at home and work, bad business decisions, and even bankruptcy, but he'd never had to watch anyone die.

"Well, it's a challenge each day, I can tell you that. And it's not likely the transplant will come before she says good-bye."

"I'm sorry," he stuttered. "She's a great girl. But why are you telling me this?" Al hadn't felt so emotionally disheveled in years.

"Would you please take the Christmas Jar? Take it for her? It's probably the last one she'll ever give." Laura began to tear up in both eyes and the sight made Al feel even more out of place. He'd made women cry before, but never quite like this. The moment had a foreign feeling he'd dwell on days and weeks later.

"I have a better idea. Wait here." Al positioned his crutches under his arms and swung his way toward Queen. She sat in the back seat of her mother's car, pretending not to have been watching. Al knocked on the window and she rolled it down. "I'll make you a deal."

"I'm listening," she sang.

"You keep ticking and keep an eye on my apartment.

Check my mail. That kind of stuff. If you do that, I'll accept your jar when I get home. Deal?"

"Deal!" Queen stuck her hand through the open window and he released one crutch to shake it.

"Deal," he repeated.

Moments later on the platform Laura asked, "What was that about?"

"She'll tell you."

Laura finally wiped away the tears that had been collecting on her cheeks. "Here's our number, in case you need anything." She handed him a sticky note. "Maybe you've got friends and family around. We try not to be nosy, but just in case, here you go."

Al folded the note and stuck it in his wallet. "Thanks."

Two days later, Al arrived in a strange small town in the south surrounded by other strange small towns and map dots he'd never even heard of.

The train station sat across the street from a Best Western, situated on U.S. Highway 4, only a mile or so from the center of the Christmas Jars universe: Chuck's Chicken 'n' Biscuits.

I handed the jar to my four-year-old to give to the chosen woman. She gave us hugs and many blessings. The jar we gave didn't contain much money this year, but it is not the amount that matters, it is the lesson behind the Jar.
—Molly

TEN

Hope hadn't rung the doorbell at the Maxwell home since her initial visits three years earlier when she was posing as a college student. She hadn't needed to then or now; it was the kind of home you just walked into as if you were a family member.

She practically was.

Lauren was standing in the kitchen making peanut butter and jelly sandwiches.

"Hi, there," Hope said. "Haven't seen you since the funeral." She kissed her on the cheek and snuck half a sandwich. As Hope took a bite, Lauren wiped peanut butter across the back of her hand with a butter knife.

"Thief."

"Anyone around?" Hope asked and licked the back of her hand like a cat. She even added a purr for effect.

"Nope," Lauren snickered. "I'm just in the mood for six PB&J's." She cut the last sandwich in half and placed each half-sandwich on a paper plate with four baby carrots, a celery stalk, and a peanut butter cookie.

"Hardy har har, Miss Smarty Shorts," Hope sassed. "Got the grandkids?"

"They're downstairs. Hannah and Dustin went on a lunch date."

"You're such a good grandma."

"Don't I know it."

Hope began making herself her own sandwich. "I haven't had one of these in forever. Mom used to make 'em for those all-day cleaning jobs."

"Hold that thought." Lauren carried a stack of paper plates down the stairs and was met with a chorus of "Yippees" and "I hate carrots." A moment later she returned to the kitchen and took a seat at the table across from Hope.

"Kids, kids, kids," Lauren said.

"Darn munchkins. Everyone's having them. What's the deal?"

Lauren got up, grabbed the baby carrots, and sat again. "Everyone but you."

"Yeah, yeah." Hope pulled the crust off her bread. "I've got nieces and nephews—who needs *real* kids?"

Lauren smiled. "You ready for Marianne and Nick to leave tonight?"

"You heard."

"We all did. You were probably the only one who *didn't* know."

"Figures. I don't know why they worried so much about it. This trip is a great opportunity. And it's her dream."

"She worried because she didn't want you to be alone. She wanted you to be cool with it."

"Cool with it?" Hope laughed.

"Just trying it out." Lauren smiled back. "You should be grateful she cares. A lot of people wouldn't dream of asking permission from people they love."

"True." Hope took the last bite of her sandwich.

"She was worried, trust me," Lauren repeated. "Worried about leaving you alone on Christmas and shorthanded at the diner. She loves the tradition as much as anyone."

"I know she does. She's a good woman."

"The best," Lauren agreed.

"Speaking of good women—you seen Gayle?" Hope asked.

"No, I need to call, maybe go by. I was waiting until some of her family started heading back out of town. It's probably still a mess of people. She'll need some real love from us when things calm down. Trust me."

Hope put her hand on Lauren's. "I keep forgetting this must be tough on you, too. Lots of fresh memories?"

Lauren nodded. "Yeah, lots of memories, but not all bad. As hard as it was losing Adam, I sure did feel loved that week. I suppose that's the silver lining for Gayle and me. For all widows. You find out who loves and supports you in times like these. Like you."

"Your husband died?"

Lauren flicked a baby carrot at Hope's nose and it caromed onto the floor.

Hope picked it up and ate it.

Lauren covered her eyes.

Something crashed to the floor on the other side of the house.

"Who's that? Someone in the shop?" Hope asked.

"Clark."

Even when she was angry with him, the name alone gave Hope goose bumps. "Of course."

"Still mad?"

"You might say that. He stopped by Chuck's on his way into town. All glib and fit."

"You really need to get over yourself," Lauren said and got up again to pull a bottle of ranch dressing from the refrigerator. "He's a good catch if you'd slow down."

"Hard to catch someone who is in and out of town more often than the train."

"Sigh," Lauren said, pulling a cereal bowl from the dish rack. Then she actually sighed and poured a deep pool of dressing into the bowl. "You've talked to Hannah?"

"Some."

"She and Dustin are having awfully mixed emotions about this."

"I'm sure they are. Can't blame them."

Lauren sat at the table and dipped a carrot into the dressing, biting it in half. "I know. I just want them happy, and this just isn't *making* them happy. But you know Dustin, he feels so committed to this. He'd always promised Adam he'd take over someday. Now that the business is his, though, he's discovered his heart isn't in it."

"Does he know what he wants to do?"

"He won't talk much about it because what he *really* wants is to learn to love the trade. But it's been three years. I don't know, Hope, I love him like he was my own, and I can see he's only going through the motions to keep his promise."

"Hannah sees it, too, doesn't she."

"Of course," Lauren said. "They're *so* close, and he's never had to say a word. She sees it in his eyes."

"Maybe you could make the decision for them. Tell him it's not working out. Make it easy on him."

"I've considered that." Lauren swirled a carrot in the dressing. "We'll see. Clark is giving it a serious look."

Hope took a carrot from the bag and doused it in the ranch dressing until she couldn't see any orange. She dropped the whole thing in her mouth and crunched. "Does he even know anything about furniture? Restoration? Repair? He's a baseball player. And judging from the way he swings a bat, he's not the greatest with wood."

Lauren shook her head. "You've been waiting to use that one, haven't you?"

Hope shrugged.

"Be sweet. . . . And no, he doesn't know a lot yet, but he's always been interested in it. He's been in the shop plenty over the years and used to love helping Adam when he was younger."

"Does he know anything about business?"

"Yes, that's not a problem. He's always had a mind for that and studied business in school. You should have remembered that."

Hope furrowed her brow. "Hmmm."

"Go say hi."

"Maybe later." Hope got up from the table and rinsed out the bowl.

"Come on, Hope. This is different from his other visits. This is serious. And if this works, if it's a fit, he's going to be around for a long time. The business needs him. And *we* need him. . . . Besides, he's got to know you would support this."

"Maaaaaybe laaaaater," Hope said as she swiped a cookie.

"Here, I'll give you an excuse. Take him a sandwich." Lauren quickly wiped jelly over one piece of bread and peanut butter over another. "Here."

Hope turned around with two carrots sticking from her mouth like fangs. "This OK?" she said, but one of the fangs fell to the floor.

"No!" Lauren said, reaching for it.

But it was too late; Hope tossed the carrot in her mouth. "Fine. Gimme the PB&J. Grrrr."

Adam's shop was connected through an air lock off the

kitchen. Hope stepped through it, pushed open the door, and saw Clark standing over a smoke-stained wooden headboard. He was dressed in slacks and a snug-fitting T-shirt. He had saw-dust in his hair and a yellow pencil tucked behind his ear.

Hope's mouth said, "Hi, Clark," but her arms said, "Welcome back, goose bumps," and her mind said, "Leeerowr."

I haven't found much of the Christmas spirit this year. The bright spot in my holidays has been the Christmas Jar and sharing the idea with others. We may have given a gift, but I think that we were the ones who were blessed.
—Penny

ELEVEN

S he is risen from the dead," Clark teased.

"Hilarious." She put a hand on her belly and mock-laughed. "You taking your act on the road?" Hope practically tossed the sandwich at him, but Clark wasn't expecting either the sandwich *or* the speed of delivery and caught it halfway from the floor with one hand. A piece of peanut butter and jelly crust fell to the floor.

Clark bent down, picked it up, and held it out for her.

"No, thanks," she said. "I already ate."

Clark put the crust in his mouth, and Hope exercised more self-control than she thought she possessed to keep from laughing.

Clark then took a largemouth-bass bite that consumed

about a third of the sandwich. "You know how long it's been since I've had one of these?"

"Last time you visited Lauren?"

"Yup," he said, and he took a bite even bigger than the last. A small glob of jelly clung to the corner of his mouth.

Hope walked over to the far side of the shop and admired the intricate hand-carved designs on the face of a grandfather clock. "This is gorgeous," she said.

"Agreed," Clark said. He finished the sandwich and tossed the paper towel in the trash can without wiping his mouth first. "Dustin said the owners took it to one of those antique valuation places and they told them it was German, pre-World War I, and worth a bundle. But it needed some work."

"Adam would have loved a project like this," Hope said.

"Probably."

Hope turned the hour and minute hands to twelve. "Is Dustin doing the work on it?"

"He'll do the wood and deep cleaning on the case. But someone else will come in and work on the mechanism itself. He tells me he's got a clock guy."

"A clock guy?"

Clark raised his hands up and shrugged his shoulders. "Who doesn't have a clock guy anymore, right?"

"Duh, right," Hope said. "I've got two. One just for weekends." She considered telling Clark he still had strawberry jelly in the corner of his mouth, but decided not telling him was much more fun.

Clark pulled a stool out from underneath a workbench and slid it toward her.

She sat, remembering sitting on the very same stool the first day she met with Adam in the shop.

Clark dropped into Adam's old rolling office chair and a cloud of sawdust puffed up around him.

"I can't believe Dustin hasn't replaced that old nasty thing," Hope said. "It's a giant piece of sawdust."

"Maybe that's why he hasn't," Clark mused. "It's not a piece of sawdust, it's a piece of Uncle Adam."

Hope looked down at her feet and kicked her heels against the legs of the stool. After a long, awkward silence she finally said what she'd been thinking since Labor Day. "You really hurt my feelings, you know."

"Oh, please," Clark said. "The picnic thing?"

She continued examining her shoes.

"Not just that, though drenching me in front of my friends at the paper—including my boss—was definitely a new low for you."

"What else then?"

She looked up.

"What?" he repeated.

Hope sighed.

"This is how it's going to be, then? Every time I come around?"

"Not if you'd quit coming and going like a bad cold."

Clark took a turn at an overdramatic sigh. "Last time was

— 78 —

different, Hope, I had a real shot at making that club in Tennessee."

"You always have a real shot at making some team somewhere—Tennessee, Virginia, Texas, Florida, blah blah blah. You zoom into town, we have dinner, I remember how much I like being in the same room with you, we go for a drive, then you drive out of town again."

Clark spun a full circle in his chair. "Let's start again, all the way from the top. . . . It's good to see you again, Hope. I'm sorry about your friend, Hope. I'm sorry I chucked you in the river, Hope. I'm sorry I ruined your shiny sneakers, Hope. I'm sorry I didn't come back to apologize for being a jerk before leaving to take the best shot I'd had all year of living my dream and getting a permanent slot on a team with a path to the Majors, Hope."

"You done?"

Clark rarely embarrassed himself. "Yes."

"Want to try that again?"

Clark spun the chair once again as if to rewind. "It *is* good to see you, Hope." He slowed his pace. "I am sorry about Chuck. Truly. And I acted like a fool when I saw you last. I'm sorry. I'm also sorry I didn't say good-bye—again."

Hope finally smiled enough to throttle down the tension. "And?"

"And I owe you a pair of shoes." He kicked playfully at one of her feet with one of his.

She kicked him back and wished she didn't enjoy the snarky reunions quite so much. "So how did it go?" she asked.

"What?"

"Baseball in Tennessee."

"I hit .169 with two homeruns and sixty-nine strikeouts in thirty-five games."

"Even *I* know that's not good," Hope jabbed.

Clark gave her his "you're killing me" look.

She'd seen it before. "I'm sorry, Clark. You'll get there."

"Oh, I don't know about *that*. Shoot, I don't even know where 'there' is anymore. Maybe *there* isn't at the ballpark. Maybe it's *here*."

"Here?" Hope asked.

"Maybe." Clark looked across the room. "You must know what's up. You and Hannah are too close *not* to. This just isn't what Dustin thought it would be, but it's tough to admit that. I know. And of course he doesn't want to feel like he's letting Adam down. Which I also understand."

Hope studied her sneakers again.

Clark watched her.

"So why you?" Hope looked up to ask. "You think you can handle this small-town life?"

"Hmmm. A loaded question if ever you've asked one." He leaned back and rested his feet on the desk. "I loved Uncle Adam. He was my dad's best friend. I know Dad would love to take over, keep it in the family, but he's too old for this. Bad back, bad knees, two mortgages on a house two hundred miles away. It breaks his heart he can't help more with it."

"Enter Clark to save the day."

"Hardly. You know I wasn't looking for this. It's just happening. But I gotta admit that being here feels comfortable."

"Here right now or here in general?"

"Both," he answered. "And maybe I see Restored like a cousin I never knew well enough or never saw enough." Clark dropped his feet to the floor and walked over to the circular saw. "Being here feels like I'm getting to know him all over again."

Hope stayed on her stool with her back turned. With the grief and heavy days following Chuck's death, she had forgotten just how much she still missed Adam, too.

Clark pulled a brush from a nail hook and swept dirt and dust off the saw.

Hope got up and walked to the other side of the room. "Do you even know how to use all this stuff?" She again nearly told him of the jelly on his mouth, but the flecks of sawdust coating it made it even more fun to look at.

"Most of it. My dad has a small workshop at home. Nothing like this, obviously, but he made me a couple baseball bats I used in college. He never wanted me to use metal. Said if I used wood bats as an amateur I'd be ready for the pros. . . . Anyway, he's always loved working with wood. He's very good with his hands. Hopefully good hands run in the family."

"I guess we'll find out," Hope said and instantly regretted it.

"Will we?"

"I didn't—"

"Forget it." Clark gently poked her in the ribs with the brush before returning it to its hook.

"Ay yi yi," Hope mumbled and walked toward the door. "I better let you get back to it."

"Hope?" Clark called.

She turned, still feeling surprisingly flushed. It was an unusual feeling for a woman who prided herself on never being flustered. "Yeah?"

"I need some help."

"With . . ."

"Getting to know the layout here, all the personalities. I know Hannah, but I don't really know Dustin very well. I need someone to help me cut through the . . . I don't know, the sawdust, I guess. Someone to guide me through what makes this place—the family, the town, all of it—tick. Make sense?"

"I think so. But you know I can't make a decision for you."

"Obviously."

"And I won't pressure you one way or the other."

"Of course."

"And I'm *really* busy right now. I've got my column. I'm keeping an eye on Gayle. Plus it's Christmas Jars time at Chuck's. So I don't know how much time I'll have to hang out and gossip."

Clark stepped toward her. "You need more help?"

"We can always use more hands. There's a lot to do."

"Rumor says I'm good with mine."

Hope covered her face. "Ugh. You're pressing repeat on that forever, aren't you?"

Clark smiled and extended his hand. "Let's make a deal. You give me some time and some inside knowledge into the family, Aunt Lauren, her quirks, the town, whatever, and I'll be your right-hand man for your little Christmas Jars project."

Hope tapped a foot and crossed her arms. She looked down at his hand, still hanging in midair to seal the deal. "OK, done." They shook hands very professionally.

Hope turned for the door, but before disappearing through the air lock and back into the kitchen, she called over her shoulder, "You might use that hand to wipe the jelly off your mouth."

Clark wiped off the jelly with his index finger and laughed loudly. Then he licked it off and laughed again.

I am left speechless. With all we have dealt with over this last year, this truly came to my family as a blessing. My thoughts and prayers go to the anonymous givers. They truly have blessed me in being able to provide my children a holiday.
—J.C.

TWELVE

L eaving at sunrise on your honeymoon by train. *So* romantic."

Marianne hugged Hope. "All Nick's idea. Every detail."

Hope had convinced Hannah, the twins and their mother, Lauren, and their husbands, and even Gayle to send off Marianne and Nick on their thirteen-year-delayed honeymoon.

Only Clark was missing.

Hope noticed.

Always the emcee in any crowd, Hope gathered everyone on the train platform in a tight circle and stood between the honeymooners. "We couldn't send you off without a few things to remind you of home while you're a gigshmillion miles away."

"Gigshmillion?" Hannah laughed.

"Hush, girl. This is my show." She put a finger to her lips, and when she pulled it away, she quickly stuck her tongue out.

Hannah returned the gesture.

"As I was saying," Hope continued, "we brought gifts. Hannah, you first."

Hannah pulled a wooden Restored, Inc. luggage tag from her pocket. "Dad made these one year for Christmas. *By hand.* He gave them to his repeat clients."

"It's lovely," Marianne said. Then she handed it to Nick who immediately replaced her suitcase tag with the new version.

The twins presented Nick with a tiny stuffed Christmas tree with a gold star sewn on the top. "Marianne won't admit it, but she's going to get homesick," one of them said. "And when she does, you pull this out."

"And she'll be even *more* homesick," Nick said and the rest laughed.

"All aboard!" the conductor yelled.

The twins' quiet husbands, Tyson and Braden, never known as big huggers, gave both Nick and Marianne a hug good-bye and wished them well.

Marianne caught her breath. "You boys are so sweet. Thank you."

Lauren came next. She reached into a bag at her feet and pulled out two leather-bound journals and two ink pens in thick, dark wood cases. She handed a set to both of them.

"Oh, my," Marianne gasped. "They're exquisite."

"These are journals Adam and I bought in San Antonio years ago. The pens were—"

"Made by him?" Marianne interrupted.

"Good guess," Lauren answered and they hugged tightly.

"All aboard!" the conductor called for the second time.

Nick picked up the bags.

"Wait!" Hope said. "Gayle and I have something."

Gayle handed Marianne a small box. "Open it on Christmas Eve in Jerusalem." When they hugged, Gayle whispered in her ear, "It's a cross pendant."

Thank you, Marianne mouthed back to her through heavy-laden tears.

Nick took Marianne's hand. "Your chariot awaits, Princess."

"We'll miss you," Hannah said, hugging both Marianne and Nick good-bye. "Christmas at Chuck's won't be the same without you."

Marianne turned to Hope. "She's right. You're sure you don't want me to stay?"

"Please. You're at the train station. Your groom is holding your bags. Get outta here."

"I just feel so—"

"Go!" Hannah and Hope both pushed her playfully from behind.

"I'm going, I'm going," Marianne said as Nick took her hand and led her up the steps to the train.

The small crowd blew kisses and waved, and Marianne disappeared into the train car. Suddenly Hope called out, "Wait!

Wait! Your jar!" But the train had begun to roll slowly down the tracks.

Marianne opened her window.

Hope ran alongside, holding an empty Christmas Jar with Chuck's distinctive label on the bottom. "Fill this there and give it away in Bethlehem!" Hope shouted as she delivered the jar through the open window into Marianne's outstretched hands.

"We will! Thank you!" Marianne blew another round of kisses to the laughing gaggle of friends and family on the platform. They waved back and stayed until the train disappeared down the tracks.

Across the street, Aaron "Al" Allred watched the scene unfold through a frosted window at his table for one and ate his free continental breakfast at the Best Western.

A Mason jar full of coins epitomizes the spirit of the holidays and will be forever cherished in this family.
—Courtney

THIRTEEN

Many drive-by diners had mused aloud how, even during the thickness of summer, it always felt like Christmas at Chuck's Chicken 'n' Biscuits. But those same patrons needed to see the diner on any given night between Thanksgiving and Christmas. The energy was palpable, even to the most hardened Scrooge.

Decorations adorned every inch of every counter and all four corners of every window. Lights in red, green, white, and gold. Fake snow piled everywhere there wasn't a stove to set it on fire. Three-and-a-half nativity scenes of varying sizes, including one whose donkey had been replaced by a plastic chicken. Most passers-by thought it was distasteful to leave up, but the one with his name on the restaurant thought it was perfect. "The chicken stays," Chuck had said in mock sternness each time someone protested.

Even the menus were decorated with special cover inserts. Each year Chuck invited children who ate at the diner to color a picture of what Christmas meant to them. They drew Christmas trees, snowmen, snowflakes, snow angels, and the occasional baby Jesus playing in the snow. Then Chuck or Gayle would insert the construction paper drawings into the plastic sleeve on the front of each menu. It was a tradition that had started, quite coincidentally everyone noted, the year Hope was discovered as a newborn in Louise's favorite booth.

Hope decided to stay busy the night Marianne and Nick left for Israel. "Just in case," she told Gayle, "something weird happens and I miss that crazy old lady."

Gayle swatted her behind with a menu.

"This is going to be a tough one for both of us, isn't it, sweetheart?" Gayle said as she handed her a dry-erase marker. Weeks earlier someone had written "The Board" in thick, alternating red and green block letters at the top of the four foot by two and a half foot dry-erase tote board that hung on the wall. It had been called the Board ever since.

"You haven't been alone on Christmas since the year Louise died."

"That's right," Hope said as though she hadn't realized it. In truth, she'd been processing that fact since the moment Marianne announced her journey to Israel. "I'm glad I have you."

"And I'm glad I have *you*," Gayle said.

Hope erased the number on the Board with a napkin. "What's the new total again?"

"Two ninety-nine."

Hope wrote the number in bold, fat lines just below the words: *Goal: 1,001.*

"Think we'll make it?" Gayle asked.

"I sure hope so. If ever there was a year to break the record, it's this one." Hope turned from the Board to find Gayle sitting at the counter, cradling her face with her tired hands. "Gayle?" Hope sat next to her on a red stool. "Gayle? Are you OK?"

The newly-minted widow nodded, breathed deeply, but kept her hands over her eyes.

"It's alright," Hope said. She put her arms around Gayle and placed her head against her friend's shoulder. She felt Gayle's upper body quivering.

"I know it's hard," Hope offered. "I know. I know."

Gayle's breathing didn't slow and it sounded as though she was struggling for air.

"Let it out. It's OK, Gayle. You know I'm here for you. We're all here for you."

A woman and her husband approached, but Hope waved them off.

Gayle finally pulled her hands away from her face and wiped her eyes and nose with a napkin. She never wore much makeup, but the little she'd applied that morning was not where she'd put it.

"Better?" Hope rubbed her back with one hand and put the other on Gayle's forearm.

Gayle nodded and wiped her eyes again, this time with her index fingers. "I'm sorry, Hope."

"Shush."

"I don't know where that came from. I've held it together so well the last couple of days."

"Not held *together*," Hope offered. *"Held in."*

Gayle nodded again. "You're probably right."

Hope's instinct was to say, *Of course I am,* but instead she said, "It's not hard to see you've been in defense mode."

Gayle took a long deep breath and sat up. She pulled her pretty, straight hair back behind her ears. "I've just tried to manage the sadness, I guess."

"Manage sadness?" Hope repeated. "I don't think you *manage sadness.* Certainly not when you lose your sweetheart."

"And best friend," Gayle said.

"That's right. And best friend." Hope got up and walked around the counter. She poured a glass of ice water for Gayle and placed it in front of her.

As Gayle took a long drink, Hope watched as a couple walked in the door with a little girl between them. The parents were Caucasian, but the girl was obviously Asian, and as adorable a child as Hope had ever seen.

Eva greeted them and motioned to a booth.

"Actually, we're here to leave this." The husband pulled a small jar from a brown paper bag. "Is Hope Jensen here?"

Hope, hearing the exchange, widened both her bright eyes and her attractive smile. She moved toward them.

"Hi, I'm Hope Jensen." She shook the parents' hands, then bent down and shook the girl's hand, too.

"I'm Pete and this is my wife, Kim."

"My name is Hannah Joy!" the girl chirped.

"Hi, Hannah. My best friend in the whole world is named Hannah."

"Really?" the girl asked, her mouth open wide. "I'm your best friend?" Her curious eyes were locked on Hope's.

"No, dear, I meant *another* Hannah."

Hannah Joy's expression fell like a vase to the floor.

"But she's just a boring grown-up," Hope recovered. "You can be my best *kid* friend named Hannah."

Hannah Joy's countenance brightened once again. "Awesome!"

Hannah's mother patted her sweetly on top of her head.

"We heard you on the radio the other day—yesterday maybe?" Pete said to Hope, and his wife, Kim, nodded in agreement. "We've had a jar on our kitchen counter, another on our dresser, and another on top of the washer for years. We've been collecting money for Hannah's college fund. But when we heard you on the radio, we thought, why not? This must be a better use of it."

"Oh, you don't need to do that," Hope said, admiring the jar in Pete's hands. "Your daughter's education is an excellent cause."

Kim took the jar from her husband's hands and placed it in Hope's. "It wasn't our idea, Ms. Jensen, it was Hannah Joy's. She was in the car when we heard you talking about your ministry here and how a Christmas Jar can bless someone. Even change their lives. She insisted that we gather all the coins and bring the jar to you."

Hope knelt in front of Hannah Joy. "Is that true, sweetheart?"

"Yep!" Hannah Joy blurted proudly. "We don't need it like someone else does."

Pete put his arm around his wife and gave her a squeeze. They exchanged a can-you-believe-how-lucky-we-are glance.

"Why won't you need it, Hannah Joy?" Hope asked.

"Because Mee Mee says I'm so smart, I'm going to get ships."

Hope looked up at Pete and Kim.

"Scholarships," Kim laughed.

"I bet you will," Hope said, tapping Hannah Joy on the nose. She stood again and examined the jar. "We'll be sure this jar gets placed with just the right family on Christmas Eve. In fact . . . you know what?" She bent down again to Hannah Joy's level. "I know *exactly* which family I'm going to bless with your jar. They have a little girl just like you but not very much money for gifts."

Kim and Pete shared the look again and Hannah Joy pulled on her mother's hand. "Can we eat now? I'm *starving*."

Hope led them to a table, handed them menus, and

thanked them profusely for the jar. Then, while they waited for their chicken platters and tots, Hope led Hannah Joy to the Board. Hope helped her onto a chair and assisted as the little girl replaced the numbers 299 with 300.

"That was fun!" Hannah Joy said.

"Sure is!" Hope said as she looked up at the Board. "Watching that number grow is the very best thing about Christmas."

We received the most amazing, thoughtful gift in the entire world last night—a large jar of coins. I was speechless and in tears for fifteen minutes. I have no idea who our "angel" is, but we are truly blessed to have such a special person watching over us.
—Nicki

FOURTEEN

The hotel pillows were so thin Al needed to stack three of them to get any measurable elevation for his leg. He'd slept better than expected both nights he'd been in town and couldn't decide whether to attribute that to a comfortable bed or still feeling exhausted from the train. *Or maybe I'm just plain old,* he thought.

After a day of watching sports on television and three kung fu movies, Al was ready to venture into town and make his way to Chuck's Chicken 'n' Biscuits. At 10:30 A.M. he called the front desk and asked for a cab. Fifteen minutes later they called back and Al swung his way to the lobby on his metal crutches.

"Where to?" the cabbie asked as Al plopped into the back seat.

"Downtown."

"More specific?"

"I don't really know. I want to end up at Chuck's Chicken 'n' Biscuits, but I'd like to see the town first."

"My pleasure," the cabbie answered, and Al realized he might have just met the only cab driver in America who wouldn't have answered with the words, "What do I look like, a tour guide?"

"Name's Tracy," the cabbie said, turning toward town on U.S. Highway 4. "What brings you to town?"

"Vacation."

Tracy nodded and looked at Al in the rearview mirror. "Excellent. Don't get many vacationers in December. You from the city?"

Al smiled. "Not exactly." He watched out the window as they passed Rhode's Family Bakery, Plaugher's Pizza and Pie, a drive-in movie theatre, and a TV station with two white vans in the parking lot with "Channel 29" painted across the sides in bright blue paint.

Tracy stopped at a light, and Al watched as two women in front of an industrial park forced a cardboard box into the back seat of a car that said "Clean Police."

"Mind if I ask about your leg?"

"I took a spill."

Tracy looked at Al again in the mirror. The light turned green. "Must have been some spill."

"Ice."

"Ouch."

"On stairs."

"Ouch!"

"Running at full speed."

"Wow!" Tracy covered his mouth to keep from laughing. "Oh, buddy, I'm sorry, I don't mean to laugh." He laughed anyway.

"That's alright," Al said. "My fault. I was in a rush."

"They get it all fixed up for you?"

"I figure we'll see. I'm full of metal right now." Al looked back over his shoulder as they passed a driving range; he wondered how long it had been since he'd held a golf club.

Tracy wanted to ask what kind of person goes on vacation after breaking a leg, especially to someplace without a beach. "Ever been to Chuck's?" he asked instead.

"Never."

"You're in for the best chicken you've ever had. I mean it. Most of the locals will tell you it's *all* about the chicken, but for me *everything* he makes . . . well, used to make—you heard Chuck passed on recently?"

Al lied, but he wasn't sure why. "No, sorry to hear that."

"Sad times. Died Thanksgiving. Right in the kitchen. Good man, he was. I heard the funeral was something else."

Al realized the lights were now closer together and the buildings were growing slightly taller with each new block, but he couldn't see anything taller than eight or ten stories across the skyline.

"Chuck's wife, Gayle, my oh my, there isn't a finer woman

in town. Such a good woman, she is." Tracy looked at Al again. "I don't think I got your name."

"Al."

"Good to meet you."

Al wasn't sure of much anymore, but he was sure Tracy meant it.

The rolling tour continued in and around town. Tracy pointed out the historical sites, the hotspots, the radio stations—two of them—the schools, and Andie O's Steakhouse, the one he claimed people drove all day and night to visit. "Chuck's is still the best deal in town, you can quote me on that, but Andie serves up the best steak you'll find anywhere. And I mean *anywhere*. Eat here before you leave town; your stomach won't regret it."

They drove on to the far side of town and passed the telephone company, a newspaper called *The Daily Record,* several small strip malls, and a community college campus.

"That's Mayor Oringdulph's house." Tracy slowed and pointed at a gorgeous antebellum mansion on a hillside.

"Oringdulph?"

"Strange name. Great mayor."

A mile later Tracy pulled to the shoulder and rolled to a stop. "That's city hall." Tracy nodded to a brick building sitting in the back of a spacious courtyard which was filled with a nativity scene and a tall Christmas tree secured with ground wires. "Come by here at night while you're in town. This spot lights up something special."

"Maybe I will," Al said.

"Christmas still means something in this town. But maybe you know that already."

"Why do you say that?"

"If it's December and an out-of-towner wants to go to Chuck's, it's usually about jars."

"Hmmm."

"Christmas Jars. It all goes down at Chuck's every year. Ever heard of it?" Tracy tried to make eye contact with Al in the mirror, but Al was staring out the window and wondering how Queen was doing.

Couldn't hurt to call and check in on my mail, he thought.

They rode quietly around the other side of town in a loop that took them back to U.S. Highway 4 and toward Chuck's. Tracy pulled in the parking lot and into the last open space. He turned around to face Al.

"Here you go. Almost noon. Get ready for some chicken and tots you won't soon forget."

"Thanks, Tracy." Al looked at the cab's meter: $86.90. "Uh-oh, I guess I lost track of the meter. I'm not sure I have that much on me—"

"Oh, don't worry about it. That's more of a guideline. I own the cab."

"How much then?"

"How about a twenty and a chicken-leg-and-thigh platter?"

"Really?"

"Sure. And you have to call me if you need to get anywhere else around town while you're here."

"Deal." Al handed him two ten-dollar bills and hopped out of the cab. He reached back for his crutches and Tracy helped him through the front door of Chuck's.

Al stepped into a wonderful cloud of smells and sights unlike anything he could have imagined from pictures and prose on a web site.

Eva, Chuck's all-time favorite waitress, greeted them at the door with a menu, an accent, and a smile.

She showed them to a corner booth and promised to bring them some sweet tea.

"Let me see if Gayle is around," Tracy said and he walked over to the register. Eva was hugging a woman good-bye and thanking her for a generous tip. A moment later Eva walked through the swinging door and into the kitchen.

Tracy returned to the booth to find Al studying a menu. "Listen, friend, you don't need this. I'll order for you. You mind?"

Al shook his head. "Not at all." He opened his jacket pocket and retrieved a bottle of pain pills. His tea arrived and he downed his midday dose of two painkillers. He returned the bottle to his jacket pocket and looked up to see Eva and Gayle approaching their booth.

Eva wore an uninteresting waitress' uniform with a white name tag engraved with her name and a cartoon chicken.

Gayle wore a white turtleneck under a forest-green sweater

with smooth black slacks. Her hair was straight; an unusual style, Al thought, for a middle-aged woman. But it fell well on her shoulders. Her makeup was light but stylish. Her perfume the same. Her eyes were tired but friendly.

Tracy stood and hugged Gayle. "Gayle, this is my new friend, Al. He's visiting."

Al tried to stand, but Gayle spotted the crutches on the floor under their table and quickly put her hand on his shoulder. "No need, but thank you. We got you in that booth, but we might not get you out again. Let's not take any chances." Her smile was a shade shy of bright, but more than could be expected for a woman still mourning her husband.

"Thank you," Al said and he shook her hand. "Al Allred. A pleasure to meet you."

"All mine. Welcome to Chuck's. We love visitors."

"I can tell."

"What brings you to town?" Gayle asked.

"Just passing through. For now. Mostly hunting for better weather than Idaho."

Gayle grinned. Al watched over her shoulder as someone from across the diner wiped numbers off the Board and replaced them. When the person turned around, Al recognized the smile from the photos on the web site.

"Hope," Gayle called, "come meet someone."

Hope put the marker down and strolled confidently to the booth.

"This is Al, he's visiting in town. First time at Chuck's."

They shook hands. "Welcome. I hope you brought a full jar."

Tracy and Gayle both laughed. "You're shameless," Gayle said.

"What? That's a big goal over there." Hope nodded toward the Board. "A thousand and one? Think that will happen easily?"

It was obvious to everyone but Al that Hope was teasing.

"I don't have a jar," Al apologized. "I'm sorry."

"Hang on," Hope said and she bolted to and from a display of empty jars behind the register with their signature label on the front. "You do now." She set it on the table in front of Al.

"Don't pay her a wink of attention," Gayle said and tugged playfully on Hope's ear. "She's our Christmas Jar missionary."

"More like nun," Hope added.

Gayle laughed again. "Don't make me call Marianne." Gayle looked back at Al. "I wish I could chat but I've got to run back to the back." She reached for and shook Al's hand one more time. "Good to have you here. And if I know this girl, she'll have you volunteering before your tots cool off."

Al said good-bye and watched the two women walk arm-in-arm back through the swinging doors. When he looked longer than Tracy thought appropriate, the cabbie grabbed his attention. "That was nice, huh? Nice of her to come out and say hello."

"Yes, indeed. Very nice."

The point is, someone cared enough to give us a Christmas Jar. Giving is the point of the Christmas Jar. It's not a lot of money, but our intention is they know someone cared enough to give it.

—Leona

FIFTEEN

Hope's evening was unusually free. She'd finished her latest edition of "Hopeful Words," her column in *The Daily Record,* and had caught up on laundry and cleaning the night before.

Marianne and Nick were already in the Middle East but hadn't called to check in since their layover in Munich. Hope considered calling them, but reminded herself that this was their honeymoon, after all.

Gayle was having a private family dinner at home with her boys. Their first since Chuck died.

Hannah, Lauren, and the twins were Christmas shopping a hundred miles away on a Girl's Night Out. They'd said they'd be home late that same night, but Hope and half the town knew they would find a hotel near the outlet stores and make one last pass through the shops before heading home. Hope regretted not accepting their invitation to tag along. She wasn't a fan of the long drive, but she loved the outlets as much as anyone. Not to mention spending time with the girls.

Hannah's husband, Dustin, was probably still at the shop with Clark. They'd been glued together of late as Clark absorbed the legacy and intricacies of Restored, Inc. Clark was staying with the Maxwells in Lauren's spare bedroom and, as far as Hope knew, hadn't even left the property since arriving in town.

Maybe he's too busy, she thought. *I bet he doesn't even remember asking me to help give him a run of the land.*

"I bet they're both hungry," she said aloud. "Working hard all day . . . well, *of course* they're hungry. Lauren's not there to make them eat." *Men are so helpless,* she thought.

She opened the fridge. *Sandwiches? No. Warmed-up Chinese? Yuck, Hope, even you wouldn't eat that.* She shut the fridge too hard and her Chuck's Chicken 'n' Biscuits magnet hit the floor. "Well, duh," she said to the cartoon chicken on the magnet.

Hope changed her clothes, brushed her hair, changed her shirt again, brushed her teeth, and put lotion on her hands and elbows. Then she made a very familiar drive to Chuck's for three box-dinners and then to the Maxwells and their adjacent shop.

Hope was surprised to find the front door was locked. *Odd,* she thought. She looked through a window but the house was dark. The doorbell hadn't worked since long before Adam died.

Hope knocked on the door and waited. She knocked again. Nothing. She stepped off the porch and walked around the side of the house to the shop. Restored's white pickup truck was parked in its usual spot. Hope peered through the window of the shop's customer door and saw what she guessed were Clark's legs poking out from underneath an antique pedestal desk. The door was unlocked and she quietly pushed it open.

"Hello there," she said, standing in the doorway. The shop was gray, and she wondered why Clark and Dustin didn't have the overhead light on. Either she hadn't been heard or she was being ignored. She chose to presume the former. "Hey there," Hope tried again, but the legs didn't move.

She scanned the shop for signs of life elsewhere. There were none. *Just me and the legs,* she thought. She casually kicked at one of the feet to get the legs' attention.

THUMP!

"Goat cheese!" a voice yelled and the head belonging to the legs swung to the side and into view.

"Oops," Hope said, holding a plastic bag of chicken dinners in one hand and her mouth with the other. "Sorry!"

Clark rubbed his forehead and stood up. He had an iPod sticking out of his front jeans pocket and ear buds in his ears. He pulled them out. "That's gonna leave a mark," he quipped.

"Yeah, about that, sorry, again, really. I didn't think that through, I guess."

"Clearly not."

"Speaking of knots. You've got one."

Clark put his hand on his forehead. A bump was forming dead center just below his hairline.

"It's not that bad," Hope said.

"If you're a unicorn, maybe."

Hope pressed her lips together to keep from laughing. "I'll get some ice."

Clark hit the light switch and ruffled his hair to dislodge the sawdust.

Hope returned with three or four ice cubes wrapped up in a paper towel.

Clark looked incredulous. "Really? *Really?* You've never made an icepack?"

"Sorry. I'm not much of a nurse."

Clark smiled and put the already-drenched ball of melting ice on his forehead. "It'll work."

Hope lifted the plastic Chuck's bag in the air. "I brought dinner for you and Dustin."

Clark looked left then right. "No Dustin. Just me tonight."

"I thought he was here."

"He was—*two hours ago.* He left to get his kids from the sitters since Hannah and the others are out shopping."

Hope felt foolish for not realizing Dustin would have been home tending to his children. "Dumb outlet shops," Hope said. "They're like magnets for those girls."

"Not you?"

"Yikes, no. You couldn't pay me enough to fight that mob for Christmas gifts."

Clark squinted his eyes, but Hope couldn't tell whether he was sizing up her white lie or wincing from the pain. Clark put the ice back on his forehead. "I'm definitely hungry though, may I?"

"Of course." Hope pulled two box-dinners from the bag and handed them to Clark.

He cleared off Adam's old desk, and Hope dashed into the kitchen for two sodas, silverware, and napkins.

When she returned they sat and Clark asked about Hope's day.

Hope asked about Clark's.

Hope asked about Clark's weekend plans.

Clark asked about hers.

Clark thanked her for the dinner and said he hadn't eaten since a very early lunch Lauren made before she scurried out of town with the girls.

Hope asked if he liked his dinner.

"Oh, yeah," Clark answered. "This chicken is amazing."

Hope agreed.

They ate silently for a moment more before Clark said what both had been thinking.

"This is weird, isn't it?"

"A little," Hope smiled.

"Why?"

"Good question," she answered. "Maybe it's the giant horn on your head."

"Oh! Ah! So funny! My pain is a joke to you. Wonderful." He put his hand on the bump again to check its size.

"It's not that bad," Hope said.

"Not that bad? I could hang things on this."

"That's what I mean, it's not that bad. Think of all the uses." Hope tried not to laugh, but the effort to hold it in caused her to cough and a tiny piece of chicken flew out of her mouth and onto the desktop between them.

Clark pinched his fingers, threatening to lift and eat it. He flicked it at her instead. "Even *I* have my limits," he said.

As they ate their chicken, tots, and rolls, they reminisced about their on-again-off-again romance. Hope wondered aloud why their timing had always been so terrible.

Clark wondered silently why more than once he'd chosen to quit Hope instead of baseball.

"What is it about us?" Hope asked, though it was directed as much at herself as it was at Clark.

"You said it. Timing."

Hope shrugged.

"Different dreams. We both wanted the big time. But I wanted to play for the New York Mets and you wanted to play for the *New York Times.*"

"True." Hope remembered the occasions they'd teased one another about who would make the move to the Big Apple first.

"Baseball's been my dream since high school. You know that. Heck, everybody knows that, right? But now I can't even get an everyday roster spot with the Class A River Bandits."

"If it makes you feel any better, I'm no closer to working for the *Times* than you are playing in the Majors."

Clark took another drink of his soda and bent the metal

ring on top back and forth until it broke off. "What does that make us then? Two dreamers with bigger dreams than talent?"

"I hope that's not true. Maybe our dreams just haven't been the right ones. I'll admit I still think about that life. Living in NYC, taking the subway to the paper, writing columns at a messy desk in the bullpen and getting lost in the shouts about deadlines and edits. Seeing my name and picture above a column read by millions. . . . All I really have so far is the messy desk and a column read by hundreds."

"And I have a swing made more for batting cages than the Big Leagues."

"But," Hope quickly added, "I've become very content in this world I live in. I love the paper and the people I work with there. The circulation may be small, but the readers are wonderful, and more people are reading my stuff every week. So maybe my dream is fine, I just need to dress it differently." She looked Clark in the eye. "What about you? Can *you* really be happy here with slightly altered dreams?"

"We'll see," Clark said, but just as he started talking again, he accidentally belched. "Oh, no. That. Just. Happened. Sorry."

"Please. That was so weak it wasn't even worth an apology."

Hope waited a moment for Clark to continue his thought, but when he didn't, she switched gears, reminiscing about meeting the Maxwell family for the first time and getting a tour of the shop. She told Clark that she'd never met anyone who loved his job as much as Adam had loved his.

"I get that," Clark said. "I've been here before to visit and when Mom and Dad would walk in the front door, Uncle Adam would grab me and pull me out here to the shop." Clark smiled and looked up at the ceiling. "Oh, man, I'd forgotten about this. One time I came here to make a Pinewood Derby car because Uncle Adam told me I couldn't lose with his help."

"You made a what?"

"You've never heard of a Pinewood Derby?"

Hope didn't have to say no, her crinkled face did the talking for her.

"That's an embarrassment. Really. I don't know that this dinner can continue."

"Oh, come on, what is it?"

Clark's eyes danced at the memory. "It's for Cub Scouts—you know what scouting is, right?"

"Sure, I once wrote a column about one of the local troops."

"Good, so imagine these scouts getting together once a year to race cars they've carved out of a block of wood."

"Sounds like a million laughs," Hope giggled. She began to stuff trash into her cardboard box.

"It is if you're a young puberty-straddling cowboy!"

"Did you just say—"

"I think I did." He put up his big right hand to stop her from speaking. "Anyway . . . every kid gets a block of wood the same size. It's a kit, with matching hard plastic black wheels, nails, everything; the whole package is exactly the same so it's fair for everyone. Then you carve your car however you want to make it as fast as you can. No two cars are ever alike."

"That could be fun, I suppose."

"It's not just a race though." Clark began gathering up his own trash. "That's what Uncle Adam said. It's a *process*. Everyone gets the same resources and the same set of rules. But the kid who wins does so because he does more with what he was given. That's the trick."

Hope tossed both dinner boxes into a tall trash can.

"I get it. It's a level playing field."

"Exactly."

Hope examined Clark's eyes. "You're enjoying this, aren't you?"

"Dinner?"

"No, *obviously* you're enjoying dinner; you're with me. I mean you're enjoying the shop."

Clark smiled. "I'll ignore the first question on the grounds that you're full of yourself."

Hope pretended to be offended.

"I think I am. Enjoying the shop, that is. I can see why Adam loved this life. Creating things, restoring life when sometimes clients don't think the furniture is worth saving."

Hope walked toward a machine and flipped what she assumed was the power switch. "You said you were getting good with all this stuff. What about this?"

"It's a sander," Clark said. "It's a very tricky piece of equipment."

"How so?"

Clark grabbed a piece of scrap wood from a box and held it on the belt. Flecks of wood shot into the air. "Wait." He powered off the sander. "Put these on." He pulled a pair of goggles from a nail on the workbench by her waist.

"Seriously?"

"Non-negotiable."

"Fine. But my eyes are my best feature."

Clark missed her retort; he was across the shop, hunting for another pair of goggles.

He walked up behind her and flipped the switch back on. "May I?"

She turned her head. "May you what?"

"Just trust me." He picked up the piece of scrap wood again.

"Famous last words." She turned back to face the sander and felt Clark ease up close behind her.

He put his arms through hers and took her hands.

She caught her breath when she felt his on her neck.

"Take this." He put the piece of scrap wood in her right hand. Slowly he guided their hands closer to the sander. "Hold just the back of it. Trust. Let my hands do the work. The trick is movement." He moved their hands toward the sander's belt and then away, then again, and again. Each time the block of wood made contact, sawdust exploded off the piece and Hope's hands tensed. "Relax," he said.

Easy for you to say, she thought, suddenly recalling vividly how lonely she always felt the day after Clark vanished for another month of chasing baseball.

Clark moved his head to look over her other shoulder and captured the scent of what he thought might have been strawberry shampoo. After a few seconds he moved again, but took his time passing by the back of her head and breathing in the scent, knowing he'd remember it long after she'd gone home for the night.

Clark rolled the piece through her hands and smoothed the corners until all the edges rolled effortlessly along their fingertips. More time passed than either would have guessed.

"Nice, isn't it?" Clark asked. "It's energizing. Taking something rough and making it smooth. Making it beautiful. I see why Adam thought the work was so noble." Clark powered off the sander. "It's a magical process."

Hope turned around to face him but hadn't realized just how close Clark's face was to hers. She leaned back against the workbench.

"Magical." Hope removed her goggles and fixed her hair.

Clark backed up and removed his goggles, too. "Well."

"Well . . ."

"Well, thanks for dinner. That was great."

"Of course. Keep the box I brought for Dustin. Have it for lunch tomorrow."

"Thumbs up," Clark both said it and gave one.

Hope smiled and sighed. "It's late. I'm off." She moved toward the door.

"Wait."

"Yeah?" Hope turned and felt her heart hiccup.

"I owe you."

"Whatever, you do not, dinner was on me."

"Not for dinner. For the company. The conversation. I said I'd help you with your project if you gave me some insider information on Lauren and the shop."

"A man of his word—rare." She winked though she didn't mean to. "OK, Monty Hall, not tomorrow, but the next day. Meet me at Chuck's in the afternoon."

"What's tomorrow?"

"Meetings at the paper, a couple of media interviews to generate buzz, nothing big."

"Look at you—"

"Hush," she said, turning the doorknob. "See you then. We'll put you to some *real* work." She winked again. *I have got to stop doing that.*

She walked out and sauntered coolly and with confidence to her car, giving her hips a hint of extra sway, just in case Clark was watching from the window.

He was.

When I first saw it, I didn't know what to say.
I just stood there looking at it and thinking,
"Is this a dream?"
—Alicia

SIXTEEN

Al slept well again. The bed, the room, the sheets, not being in Idaho Falls—all of it contributed to more blissful sleep than he'd had in far too long.

He hopped out of bed on his good leg and grabbed the newspaper that had been slipped under his door. He hopped a few more times to the bathroom, then back to his bed where he spent an hour reading *The Daily Record*.

World news and sports news. Business news and stocks. New babies and obituaries. Wedding announcements and classifieds. But what caught his eye most was a column on the left-hand side of the front page of the Lifestyles section: "Hopeful Words," by Hope Jensen. He thought she looked much better in real life than in the photo accompanying her byline.

The column told Hope's story of meeting a slick corporate

attorney on a recent flight. The man had confided that he finally recognized he'd been operating in the gray areas of the law and life for too long. He was on his way to San Diego to look at a coffee shop for sale and planning to launch a new midlife career he could be proud of. "I've spent my career making everything personal," he told her at 35,000 feet. "Battling for my clients even when I knew we were wrong. Usually we *both* knew we were wrong. We've been fighting and scraping and dancing with the truth when we didn't need to."

Hope commended her new friend for his courage to change his life and closed the column by challenging her readers to find a mirror and stare at their reflections for as long as it took to find answers. "Am I living, working and playing with integrity? If not, what changes should I make to fulfill my destiny and find true happiness?"

Al recalled his time with Cowboy Craig. Despite his distaste for the long drives, and the fact that all his clothes smelled like teriyaki jerky, he'd been a good employee. *Good enough, anyway,* he thought.

He finished the paper and tossed it on the floor. He had only a few minutes before the free breakfast ended and bathing—his only option with the cast—was a time-consuming process. He threw on a wrinkled T-shirt and his jeans with the left pant leg cut off below the knee. It was good enough for the hotel lobby, but he was grateful he had no one to impress that morning.

The dining area was still crowded with last-minute guests filling their plates with mini-boxes of cold cereal, danishes, toast, and yogurt. Al certainly didn't have to work very hard for offers of help. He simply hobbled toward the stack of Styrofoam plates, picked one up, dropped it, and before he could have possibly bent over, a woman's voice stopped him from behind.

"Lemme git that fer yew." Her accent was rich and attractive.

He turned to see her face.

It was not.

The homely woman's smile was as kind as her voice, but to Al that was the end of her upside. Her complexion was blotchy and cratered. Her eyebrows—or eyebrow—Al noticed, was unruly.

"Can I git some breakfast fer yew?"

"I couldn't ask that, but thank you." He began to hobble toward a table.

"Yew don't have ta ask, sir, I'm doin' it." She smiled again and Al noticed at least one other highlight: a full compliment of teeth.

He sat at the nearest table and rested his crutches against a wooden column.

Two children raced into the lobby from the elevator. "Yew beat us here, Momma!" a little girl shouted.

"I sure did, honeybun. I told yew I would." The mother tickled one girl's belly when she got close.

"Lesley and Wendi, would ya sit with my friend here while I git him some breakfast?"

Al protested. "You really don't need to—" But it was too late; Southern Accent was already filling two plates.

The girls sat on either side of Al and introduced themselves. They each shook his hand and Wendi said, "Nice to meet yew, sir."

"Pleasure to meet yew, sir," Lesley added.

The girls bubbled like soda water and Al struggled to keep up with the questions. Every few seconds he checked the breakfast bar. *What's taking so long?* he thought. *Is she slaughtering the pig for a couple slices of bacon?* Then he realized she probably could.

"I'm sorry that took so long," she said, putting the plates on his table. She'd brought two kinds of toast, three boxes of cereal, 2% milk, skim milk, orange juice, two donuts, a bagel, an English muffin, jelly, butter, and three varieties of yogurt.

"I wasn't sure what yew'd want."

He thanked her.

The woman and her two children said gracious good-byes and walked away. But before they were out of range, he heard Wendi say to her mother, "That man was so nice, Momma. I sure hope his leg gits better."

Al watched the girls skip through the hotel lobby and out the automatic doors.

Then he ate so much he wished he'd written down the number for the Flab Strap.

Later in his room he rifled through his wallet and found the sticky note with the phone number for Queen and Laura's apartment.

The phone rang twice.

"Ross residence, Lara speaking."

Al hesitated.

"I said, Ross residence, Lara speaking."

"Hello."

"Hello?"

"This is Mr. Allred. Is your mother home?"

"Hi, Mr. Allred! It's Queen."

Al smiled and moved the phone from one ear to another. "Thanks, Queen. I wasn't quite sure."

She giggled. "Mom's still sleeping."

"Oh, I can call back then. It's early there."

"That's OK. *I'm* not still sleeping."

Neither spoke for a moment.

"Have you been checking my mail for me?"

"Yes, I have! Mom says you get a lot of bills like us."

Al began to laugh but caught himself. "I figure I do."

"Mom puts your mail on the counter every day. Just like you asked."

"That's nice of her," he said. He switched ears again with the phone. "And how are you doing?"

"I'm tired today. And my stomach hurts. But yesterday was a good day. Mom said I didn't have to go to the hospital so we went to the park instead."

"In the winter? Wasn't it cold?"

"It was *freezing*. But Mom said you never know when your last trip to the park might be."

"Oh."

"Mom said parks don't last forever."

Al lay back on the bed. "Your mother is right."

"Uh-oh, hold on a minute—"

In the background he heard the unmistakable sound of someone throwing up. Then he heard Queen's mother. "It's alright, Lara. I'm here now. It's alright."

The toilet flushed and as the sound faded he could tell Queen was crying. He pulled the phone away from his head and counted to thirty. Then he put the phone back to his ear.

"Hello? Are you gone, Mr. Allred?" It was Laura.

"Oh, hi. I was just hanging up. I'll call later."

"No, don't hang up, it's settled down. Queen's gone to change her shirt. . . . How much did you hear?"

"Not much." He paused. "How is she?"

"Up and down. Yesterday was up. Today is down. She's on some new medicine that's making her sick. Obviously."

"I'm sorry."

"It's fine. It's life."

"No news on the list?" He zigged.

"None."

"How's everything else?" He zagged.

"Your mail is piling up on my counter. We've not opened anything of course, but we've flipped through it and there doesn't seem to be anything scary."

"What exactly does scary mail look like?" Al asked with a light laugh.

"Well, let's see. Letters from the IRS, collections, hospital bills, jury duty notice, Halloween party invitations."

"Good point," Al said.

"How's your trip?" Laura asked.

"Good so far."

"How's the leg?"

"Better. It doesn't hurt much anymore when I don't keep it elevated."

"That's good. Crutches getting easier?"

"As easy as crutches get."

Al heard Queen reenter the room. "I like this shirt better anyway," Queen said.

"Me too," her mother said.

"Can I talk to Queen again real quick?" Al asked.

"Of course."

"Hi, again," Queen said a moment later.

"Feeling better?"

"Much better, thanks! Are you coming back to Idaho soon?"

"I don't know yet."

"Where are you anyway, Mr. Allred?"

"That's why I wanted to talk to you again. You know that Christmas Jar you tried to give me?"

"Um, yeah." She giggled.

"Go get it."

"Really? OK, don't leave." She dropped the phone on what sounded like a Formica kitchen counter. "Queen's back," she blurted fifteen seconds later.

"Look at the bottom of the jar," Al said.

"There's a sticker."

"What does it say?"

"It says, 'Someone loves you! You're holding a Christmas Jar. The miracle starts with you! www.ChucksChickenAndBiscuits .com.'"

"I'm there."

"At ChucksChickenAndBiscuits.com?"

Al laughed in a loud, healthy bellow. "No Queen, I'm at the *diner.* I'm down the street, actually, in a hotel."

"Cool."

"Your Christmas Jar came from right here. This is like the North Pole for Christmas Jars. They collect them here. Then they give them away. There's money and jars everywhere. I've never *seen* so much money."

"Cool!"

"I'm going to help them collect more jars than ever, Queen. We're going to take the idea all across America. From here all the way to Idaho. That's cool, too, right? Oh, and guess what else? They have a truck dressed up like a chicken. It has a big yellow beak on the front and when it honks it makes a 'buck buck' sound. It's called the Cluck Truck."

"*Way* cool. Maybe I could ride in it sometime?"

"I thought you'd like that. Maybe someday."

"Hmmmuhhh . . ." Her voice trailed into a long hum.

"Are you OK?"

Suddenly Queen became silent. "Uh-oh, I gotta go—"

This time Al didn't listen.

*We know the money in these jars can in no way begin
to solve this family's financial difficulties, but our hope is
they know how very much they are loved.*
—Marge

SEVENTEEN

Eva and Hope were giggling about her spontaneous wood-shop date with Clark when they looked out the window and saw a cab pull away. Seconds later Al walked in the front door of Chuck's. He wore a light blue, buttoned-down shirt under a burgundy V-neck sweater with wrinkle-free khakis he'd picked up at a department store two blocks from his hotel. Instead of cutting off the entire left pant leg to the height of his cast, he simply cut the seam to the knee. He also wore one shiny loafer.

Eva sat him at the counter and put his crutches by the coatrack.

"Nice to see you again," she said in a sincere tone. Al realized he'd nearly forgotten what sincerity from a woman sounded like.

"You got that jar filled yet?" Hope asked with a playful slap on the counter. She recognized his face immediately.

"Working on it, Hope."

"Ah, so you're good with names. I'm impressed."

"Not really." He pointed to a newspaper clipping with her photo under the glass on the counter in front of him.

"Ouch!" she said, grinning, and Al wondered if her big, healthy smile would be better suited for sales than journalism.

"Sorry. But if it helps, I would have remembered your name anyway."

"Too late," she said, slapping the counter again. "No tots for you."

Al laughed. "And do you remember *my* name?"

Hope put her palms together as if to pray and then placed her fingers against her mouth. "Let me think." She closed her eyes and hummed. "Scott? Greg? With two Gs? Tim? Buckaroo Bartholomew?"

Al shook his head.

"Don't tell me. Jason? No. Allen?"

The kitchen door swung open and Gayle appeared. "Welcome back, Al," she said on her way to the register.

Al smiled.

"Al was my next guess," Hope said.

"Uh-huh," Al teased.

"I won't forget again, Al, I promise." Hope touched his shoulder as she walked by to meet Gayle up front.

Eventually Eva returned to take his order. "Sorry about that, I'm alone today."

Al ordered a chicken sandwich and lemonade and read clippings under the glass until his food arrived. Every few minutes he stole a glance across the diner at Hope and Gayle talking. Gayle was dressed too nicely, he thought, for someone who spent so much time in a greasy southern diner. She wore a soft purple sweater over a white blouse with an oversized collar. Al thought it unfortunate that only her calves were visible below her black, knee-length skirt. Still, he decided, she was a striking woman for her age.

No, striking at any age, he corrected.

He ate his lunch as slowly as he could, partly to savor the flavor but mostly to prolong his time in the diner. He couldn't overhear them, but Hope and Gayle were in serious conversation, constantly moving back and forth from cases of jars by the Christmas Tree to a three-ring binder by the register.

When Eva cleared his plate away, Al ordered a piece of pie. After the pie was gone, he asked for a refill on his lemonade. When she checked on him again, he asked if she'd mind getting him the newspaper he saw on the table of one of the empty booths.

"You still here?" Hope said, standing across from him at the counter.

Al looked left and right and down at his hands. "Seems so," he grinned.

Hope rolled her eyes. "If you stay much longer, we'll put you to work."

"How so?" Al sat up.

"I was kidding," she said, tilting her head to the side. "But if you're offering . . ."

"Name it. I'm here to help."

"Really?"

"Yes. Name it. Happy to help."

"You don't have anywhere to be?" Hope asked.

"Not today."

Hope studied him. "You've got a story, don't you?"

"A story?"

"About a jar. A Christmas Jar."

Al looked away. "I got one, yeah—well, sort of got one, I figure—and I think the concept is brilliant." He looked back at her. "It's marketing gold."

"Go on."

"I don't want to be presumptuous, but I figure this thing, your work here, it hasn't scratched the surface. This could really become something national. Even international. It's got *so much* potential."

Hope was silent; hearing someone else talk about the same goal somehow gave it new weight.

"And if I can help, I'd love to."

Hope remained still a minute longer.

"I apologize, I didn't mean to overstep—"

"Not at all." Hope called Gayle back from the kitchen. "Good news," she said when Gayle appeared.

"What's that?"

"We have an angel among us."

"Do we?" Gayle smiled at Al.

"Al's offered to help. Shall we put him to work?"

"Yes," Gayle answered. "Yes, we should."

Hope explained that she and Gayle were leaving to make a presentation at a middle school and would be gone for several hours. But sometime that afternoon a pastor would be passing through town; he'd called at the last minute to request 150 empty jars for his congregation. He promised to encourage as many members of his flock as possible to bring their full jars back in time for Christmas delivery in order to boost their total toward the goal of 1,001.

"Here's the dilemma. Eva's busy, Randall is cooking alone, Gayle's boys are in a meeting at the bank, and all our other normally helpful hands are tied up this afternoon."

"What do I do?" Al was asking Hope, but he was looking at Gayle.

"Can you put stickers on jars and the instruction notes inside each one? Then repack them in the cases?"

"Done."

"And if you have any suggestions, like about the wording on the instructions, pipe up. Please."

"I certainly will!" Al couldn't believe how excited he sounded—and felt.

"Great. I'll set you up at one of the tables, or here if you think that works better, and put everything within reach. And if you need to leave before the guy from the church gets here . . . What's his name again, Gayle?"

"It's a woman," Gayle said. "Pastor Creasy."

"If the jars are ready but you need to leave before Pastor Creasy gets here, Eva could probably handle the handoff."

"Done. I'm happy to help the cause."

"You're a lifesaver."

Hope brought Al cases of jars, rolls of stickers, a stack of paper, a paper cutter, and a baggie full of five-inch, pre-cut strands of yarn. She demonstrated the assembly process and within minutes, Hope and Gayle were loading their own batch of jars into Gayle's car and speeding off to an assembly at a school two towns away.

Al surveyed the mountain of work he thought he'd be doing alongside Hope and Gayle. The reality of doing it alone was improved substantially when Eva whispered in his ear that Gayle had insisted lunch and refills were on the house.

Al thanked her, asked for another lemonade, hobbled to the bathroom and back, took a look at the number on the Board—378—and then spent three hours preparing Christmas Jars with intense precision and care. Each sticker perfectly centered. Each scroll of instructions cut in a perfect line. Each string tied in an immaculate bow.

They've never looked so perfect, he thought.

The only break he took was to call Queen. "You'll never believe what I'm doing right now."

Actually, she had no trouble believing at all.

It has been a difficult Christmas with our finances, but I have maintained my faith that God will provide. We were so moved to know someone considered us worthy of a Christmas Jar.
—Tina

EIGHTEEN

———•———

Sometime since Al's first visit to Chuck's Chicken 'n' Biscuits, someone had drawn a "Days Left" box in the upper right-hand corner of the Board once dedicated only to counting the number of growing jars.

It now read *Days Left Until Christmas: 8*

Al had spent nearly every day at Chuck's since his first volunteer effort to Hope's unofficial Christmas Jars ministry. He'd also changed his credit card on file at the hotel twice and applied for credit line increases on two other cards.

Tracy the cab driver often carted him back and forth in exchange for a free meal at Chuck's, something Gayle was happy to provide. Though Tracy maintained he would do it for free as his meager contribution to the mission.

When Tracy was busy hauling actual paying customers,

either Hope, Gayle, or Eva would fetch Al from his hotel or return him home at night. He was grateful for any ride, and though he enjoyed Hope's energy, he appreciated Gayle's sweet grace the most.

Al's phone calls with Queen had become a part of the evening routine every few nights. They always began with Queen answering with her now-customary, "Ross residence, Queen speaking." They'd chat briefly, then her mother would take the phone, leave the room, and report on some piece of official-looking mail or apartment-complex gossip.

Then Al always asked the question. "How is she?"

The answers varied.

"OK . . . Fighting . . . Not bad today . . . Nauseous . . . A little blue . . . Typical Queen . . . Realistic."

There was also her most recent answer: "Fading."

Queen's mother enjoyed talking to Al about her daughter because he was the only one who simply listened and didn't press for more information, give advice, fall apart emotionally, or somehow find a way to make Queen's deteriorating condition about themselves. She also enjoyed the minor distraction of keeping an eye on Al's apartment and car in the parking lot.

After the updates, Queen would take the phone back and swamp him with questions and information. "How are the Christmas Jars people doing? Tell me what jars you collected today. Did I tell you we got another jar yesterday? It's our *second* one this year and it's not even Christmas yet! Mom says people are watching over me. Mom says my job is to count the money. Her job is to pay the bills. Mom says the people at the bank hide when they see us coming with all our coins. Why would they hide?"

Inevitably Queen would run out of steam and either quietly say good-bye or simply hand the phone off to her mother.

"Thanks for being her friend," Laura liked to say. "She loves your calls because you're the only one who doesn't patronize her. Please call again."

He did. And soon the calls went from every few days to every other day to every single night.

The longer Al lingered around Chuck's, the more he found other questions to answer as well. And he'd learned to answer the why's, when's and what-are-you-doing-here's like a seasoned sales vet.

"What brings you to our small town?"

"Warmer weather, a change of pace, being part of something great."

"Why here?"

"Why not? You've got a slice of heaven here. Plus this is the home of the Christmas Jars, right?"

"Why not rent an apartment, or buy a home and put down roots?"

"I'll see how things feel after Christmas. I have options."

"Are you looking for a job? Can we help?"

"No, thanks. I used to trade in cattle and repped some of the largest ranches in the west. And I got embarrassingly lucky with investments."

"Do you have family nearby?"

"Not yet, but I feel more like family every day."

One day Al noticed Gayle's sons, Joel and Mike, sitting in a booth with an out-of-towner in the kind of suit Al used to wear, discussing the possibility of franchising Chuck's into other cities. When the man—probably an attorney, Al reasoned—finally left the restaurant, Al rode his crutches to their table and invited himself to sit.

"Do you mind?" he asked.

"Hey, Al, not at all."

"I couldn't help but overhear a touch of your meeting just now. You're thinking of franchising?"

Joel and Mike looked at each other quickly and then back at Al. "Maybe," Joel said.

"I have some experience with that. A few careers ago I helped some colleagues turn a very, very successful New York-style deli in California into a franchise model. They've got nine locations now. It's tough, but can really pay off if done right."

"I thought you were in livestock or something like that," Mike said.

"Like I said, it was a few careers ago." Al kept eye contact with Mike. "Anyway, for what it's worth, I think it's a great idea. You've got proprietary recipes people love—especially the chicken, obviously—and a very unique homegrown appeal. Plus the more the Christmas Jars thing spreads, the more your brand gets out there. I could see it working. I really could."

"Thanks, Al," Joel said.

"Think about it—every new location could be like a regional hub for our Christmas Jars work. A thousand jars here, a thousand more at the other locations . . . one helps the other, I figure, right? And if we get on one of the big shows, not radio but TV? Forget about it, you'll be bigger than Colonel Sanders."

"Huh," Joel said. "Worth a thought."

"Yeah, thanks," Mike added. "Maybe we'll hit you up for some advice sometime."

"Anytime, guys. Anytime." With that, Al stood and crutched his way back to his own table, wondering if it might be time to start pitching the idea of a TV interview to all the morning shows.

Hope and Clark were spending much more time together than ever before. They often saw each other twice a day, and often those days ended over dinner or along the many paths that followed the river on the south side of the county.

Clark kept his promise to volunteer collecting jars and Hope had him running everywhere in the Cluck Truck. "A deal's a deal," he told her when she offered to let him off the hook. And so Hope had also kept her word, filling Clark's head with anecdotes about her nearly four years of living in the Maxwell's world and spending many hours in the shop.

But their working arrangement was little more than a farce. It was true—they didn't need excuses to spend time together anymore, and they knew it. Something was happening that Hope always thought possible if they stayed in the same zip code long enough. And while it scared her, it also made her feel like what she imagined Lauren and Marianne must have felt during their courtships.

Lauren couldn't have been happier for the budding couple. She reminded Hope constantly that she and Adam knew the altar was their ultimate destination after just their first date. One evening, she went so far as to suggest she would move out of the home and sell it to Clark if he and Hope were to marry and take over the shop together.

"Lauren Maxwell!"

"Please, honey, you've spent more time with him the last few weeks than most courting couples do in year. And it's not like you haven't tested his waters before."

"I don't even know what that means!" But Hope couldn't argue the point. They'd been skiing and hiking; they'd made a kitchen table together; she'd showed him off at the newspaper. They had driven 150 miles together to pick up five jars containing cash and change totaling $4,360 from a high school that dedicated an entire semester to the project after Hope spoke to their journalism class and inspired them to the challenge. They'd even been to the batting cages, which would have been closed for the winter except the owner was Chuck and Gayle's longtime neighbor. Clark stood close to Hope and taught her the mechanics of the swing and she pretended not to understand, over and over again.

What they hadn't done was kiss. Hope gave Clark a monologue at Andie O's Steakhouse about not rushing into anything and taking any steps that would force what should be an "organic issue," as she called it. Hope meant a far more serious intimacy than a simple good-night kiss, but Clark chose the safest path and decided to test Hope's independent streak.

When she's ready, he told himself, *she'll kiss me.*

But Hope's independent personality didn't extend to matters of love, and she remained a traditionalist in the mold of her mother. The thought of initiating a first kiss with a boy would have turned Louise Jensen's cheeks Cherry ChapStick red. So he waited, she waited, and the consequence of not having a physical relationship resulted in a layered friendship Hope had never experienced with a man.

As for the kiss, Marianne would have been much more approving; and as each new and evolving emotion for Clark surfaced, Hope regretted—if only slightly—being so supportive of Marianne and Nick's holiday trip to Israel. They'd spoken by phone a few times and Hope had received dozens of pictures of the honeymooners at historical and religious sites. But the phone and e-mail wasn't the same as staying up all night at the diner and eating Three Musketeers pie while talking about boys.

Gayle was still mourning the loss of her husband, but with the holidays, the Christmas Jars work, and her sons deciding what to do with the diner, she hadn't had time to slow down quite as much as she might have wanted. Instead she smiled her way through the days, keeping busy and appreciating the extra help and attention. And after all, her husband had made her promise no tears and no languishing in grief. So her tears were saved for the early hours of the morning when her defenses were not yet mounted and the reminder of an empty bed was still very fresh.

The extra attention at the diner came from all angles. Eva had always been a trusted friend and member of the family, but their friendship had grown even closer since the funeral, and Gayle was saddened that Eva was leaving for the holidays so soon. Eva had offered to cancel her trip to visit family, but Gayle refused and promised her that Chuck would have wanted her to take the break. "The other three waitresses can pick up the slack, Eva. You trained them so well."

Eva relented and bid farewell for the holidays.

Hannah and Dustin were becoming excited about the prospect of Clark taking over Restored. Sensing it was nearly a sure thing, Dustin had started researching teaching opportunities and had already garnered some interest from the same community college Hope attended. A part-time slot, they told him, could be open as soon as mid-January.

Teaching had been Dustin's dream since his first year of college, but after falling in love with Hannah and the rest of the Maxwell brood, he decided he could love taking over the family business just as much. What he discovered was that as much as he honored and respected his father-in-law's passion and successful business, he'd rather mold young minds than old wood.

Hannah was in Hope's rearview mirror constantly asking for updates about the fledgling romance with Clark.

"Hope Jensen, you still haven't kissed? That's just wrong, girl. What is he waiting for?"

"Hope, Hope, Hope, you know how rare a love letter is? Dustin hasn't written me a letter in years!"

"Clark took you to the batting cages? In winter? He was totally showing off, right? Gosh, I love that about boys."

"Flutter-flutter. Dustin did the breakfast in the park date once, too. And look where it got us!"

"He bought you tulips? So sweet! You realize why he bought them, right? Tu-lips—get it?"

She didn't. And the closer Christmas came, the busier she was. Too busy, she thought, to decipher every nuance of Clark's brand of humor.

Lauren, too, was busier than she'd ever been. To deal with her own annual sadness of having lost her husband and best friend, Adam—also at Christmastime—Lauren filled her days with grandchildren and volunteering at the school and hospital. With what little time she had left, she nurtured Clark's interest in taking over the family business and dropped gratuitous hints of her approval of his budding relationship with Hope.

And like everyone else, Lauren spent her fair share of time at Chuck's, working alongside Hope, Al, and the rest of the team in pursuit of their lofty goal. She also spent quiet hours at night buried in journals and photo albums, pondering what Adam would think of it all.

We handed her our jar and she couldn't stop hugging
and thanking us. She said that we were her angels.
I will cherish the memories from our trip today, forever.
  —Christie

NINETEEN

I s Hope here?" A man asked as the waitress pushed two tables together for his wife and four children.

"She might still be in the back, I'll check." The waitress passed through the swinging door as the family settled in for dinner at Chuck's. The happy couple tried to keep their three boys and one girl from fighting over two menus.

"Dale!" Hope yelped as she spotted her old friend.

"Hey, stranger," Dale said. He stood and they embraced. "You remember my wife, Mary Ann."

"Of course. That's a name I can't forget." Hope smiled broadly as Dale introduced the children.

Clark, who had been in the back kitchen, came out to check on the buzz.

"We've got a surprise for you, Hope."

"Jars? You brought me jars?" Hope's voice rose.

"Not exactly," Dale replied. "But we did give away our first one tonight."

"Actually four!" One of the boys yelled much louder than his parents approved of.

"Four?" Hope said.

"Yes. I know you take jars here, too. I've been reading your columns in the paper. But we had an idea to deliver them ourselves to a family we knew had a very *unique* need. It's been a really tragic month for them."

"Tell us about it," Hope said, trying not to glance at the Board to check the number.

"It should have been Mission Possible," Dale began. "Except it turned out to be Mission *Impossible*. After arriving at the house we'd picked and carefully reviewing the escape route with the two oldest over there—they were making the actual delivery—it was go time. Right, boys?" Dale smiled at his sons before turning back to Hope. "The boys had to go it alone because I recently had knee surgery—"

"I hadn't heard that, you OK now?"

"Better, but I still can't outrun a fat snail."

Dale's children chirped at the joke.

"So Mary Ann here drove the getaway minivan. I rode shotgun. We dropped the boys off and quickly drove around the corner to the rendezvous point. After a few minutes, we saw them approaching in the darkness. My wife fired up the car for the getaway, but as far as stealth getaways go, this one was a *total* disaster. The boys were not running as planned and actually seemed to be limping. As they slowly, and I mean *slowly*, got to the car, we realized both of them were crying. With zeal!"

Dale noticed most of the other diners around them had tuned in to hear the story. He amped up the details. "We didn't have time to worry about why or what happened, we just had to get away. They opened the doors to get in the van and we started encouraging them, you know, rather loudly. Our oldest, Isaiah over there"—Dale pointed to one of his sons—"he got in the front seat and promptly slammed the door on Benjamin's arm as he was climbing into the back seat."

Hope looked at the boys; they were sword fighting with rolled-up menus.

"So now it wasn't just *crying* in the middle of the street, it was *screaming* too. And it was contagious. The baby was scared to death, so *naturally* she joined in."

Hope and Clark were both trying not to laugh, but she was more successful than he was. His hearty laugh was a Maxwell family trademark.

"Mary Ann jumped out to help corral everyone into our now *very* conspicuous van so we could complete our escape. I grabbed my son and laid down on the back seat with him on top of me, feeling sure someone was going to hear the screaming and call the police. I absolutely, positively, expected to get caught and was merely hoping the police wouldn't arrive before we drove away."

"That would have been memorable," Clark said.

Dale nodded. "Isn't *that* the truth. After a drive around the neighborhood had soothed our nerves and gave us time to check for broken bones—"

"None, thankfully," Mary Ann added.

"We finally got the story of what actually happened out there. As the boys were making their escape through the back-yard, they didn't notice a rope tied low across the back lawn. They had both tripped and fallen and made who knows how much noise."

"That's classic," Clark said. He put his arm around Hope.

"Classic is one word for it. It sure didn't go smoothly, and couldn't have gone much worse, but the night *was* a success, right, gang?"

"Right!" they clamored.

"We drove by the house later to make sure the jars were gone, and sure enough, all of the lights were on so we knew the jars were safely inside. Knowing the money was being counted and the Christmas Jar miracle had spread a little further was all we needed to know. Our boys were excited to know they had actually helped someone and we all had an experience we will never forget."

Dale's wife reached up and took her husband's hand. "I'm certain next year's delivery will go better," Dale finished, "because I think I'll hire the neighbor kid to deliver the jar while I stay safely home in bed."

"Be nice," Mary Ann teased, giving a tug to his arm hair.

"That's an awesome story, Dale," Hope said. "Thanks for coming by and sharing."

They spoke another minute or two, hugged good-bye, and then Hope and Clark excused themselves to the kitchen.

"Cool story, huh, Hope?"

"Uh-huh."

"How do you know them?"

Hope picked at her chicken.

"Hope?"

"Yeah?"

"You OK?"

"Yeah, I'm fine. . . . We went to high school together. I haven't seen him since their first was a baby. They live on a farm somewhere, I think."

"Unusual story, right? I bet you don't get many like that."

Hope was picking at her chicken again, trying to pull meat from a drumstick that was already bare.

"What's up over there?" Clark asked.

"Nothing."

"Doesn't look like nothing. You're out of it."

Hope dropped the drumstick on her plate and wiped her hands on an apron that had been balled up on the nearby prep table. "Just worried."

"Bout what?"

"That number on the Board."

"Number?"

"A thousand and one. It's a *big* number, you know?"

"Yeah, but you'll make it. *We'll* make it."

"I don't know," Hope mumbled.

Randall, the senior cook, passed between the couple on his way to the walk-in freezer.

Clark tossed his head in the direction of the back door. "C'mon," he said, and Hope followed him outside.

"It's gotten cold tonight," Clark said.

Hope exhaled and watched her breath dissipate into the thin night air.

Clark unlocked his pickup truck—a vehicle on loan from Restored—and opened the passenger's door. "Climb in."

Hope answered by gracefully easing up and into the seat.

Clark shut the door behind her. As he crossed to his side of the truck, he saw Hope blow hard on the window and draw a smiley face in the wet circle.

"Why do I get the feeling you don't actually feel that way?" Clark said as he started the truck and turned on the heat.

"Because you're an unusually perceptive male?" she said, watching the face fade away on the glass.

"I'll take that as a compliment. Even though it was insulting to a couple billion other guys."

Hope blew on the glass again and wrote the number 1,001.

"Alright Hope Jensen, what's up?"

"Oh, I dunno. Just stressed."

"Why? It's Christmas. You're happy, you're healthy, you're beautiful, you're dating a great guy. What's to be stressed about?"

"I'm dating a great guy?"

"Yes, you are." He flicked her leg with his index finger. "Don't you read the paper?"

Hope sighed again.

"You really are in a funk, aren't you?"

"I don't know that we're going to make it."

"Make what?"

"The number. The Christmas Jars goal."

"Oh. That." He felt oddly relieved. "Would that be such a crime? You're obviously working yourself to death and doing so much good with it, so who cares if you meet some arbitrary goal?"

"Arbitrary?" Hope looked at him and wished she could see his eyes better. Only a single streetlight lit the back parking lot of Chuck's and they weren't near its glow. "Hardly, it's a real number. We agreed on it. It's never been done before."

"Fine, but Hope, it's still just a *number,* right?"

She turned to him.

"A thousand jars. It's a goal, sure, but it's still just some number."

"A thousand and *one,*" she corrected and turned away from him.

"Whatever. It's just a number on a white board. If you only get to eight hundred, or nine hundred, or nine hundred and ninety-nine, it doesn't matter in the end. As long as you're helping people. As long as you're putting jars in the hands of people who need the help, right?"

Hope sighed and turned up the truck's heater. "I know, I know. You're right."

Clark reached over and took her hand.

She interlocked her fingers with his.

"But it's *important* to me, Clark. It's something I've worked toward for weeks, *months* really. It matters to me."

Clark leaned back against his headrest. *Important to me.* He repeated the words in his mind. "I can see what you mean."

Hope ambled on. "I guess it's just that Al has so many good ideas, and we don't have enough time to possibly do them all this year. But he's right when he says this is just the beginning. . . . If we handle things right, this could become bigger than any of us. A true movement. A full-time organization. Seminars. Year-round fund-raising. TV. Maybe a documentary. Partnerships. Millions of jars."

"Whoa. Millions?"

"Why not?"

"Well, it seems—"

"Daunting?" Hope squeezed his hand. "And *that's* why I like you so much. I've never been around a guy who gets me as well as you seem to." She inched closer to Clark and for the first time in weeks considered breaking Louise's cardinal rule about first kisses.

Clark also leaned in and admired the smooth lines of Hope's cheeks and perfect chin. Even in the faded light her face shone warmth he could see and feel from two feet away. He leaned in further . . .

THUMP THUMP. A fist on the window.

"Hope!" Gayle's son Mike was rapping on the window. "You've got a phone call inside the diner from *America Live*."

Hope threw the door open and jumped down from the truck. "You're kidding!"

"Nope, some guy is on the phone. Something Kincaid."

"Yow yow yow!" she yelled and raced across the parking lot and through the back door of the kitchen.

Mike poked his head into the truck's cab. "Ouch, sorry about that, man. Bad timing, huh?"

"Oh, no. You're way off base, Mike. We were just talking. That's it." Clark grinned slyly, turned off the truck and thought, *Her move.*

Inside the diner Hope picked up the cordless phone and in her best nonchalant tone oozed, "Hi, this is Hope Jensen. May I help you?"

"Hope, it's Burton Kincaid with *America Live*."

"Hello, Mr. Kincaid, what a surprise."

"Just Burton."

"Hello—" Hope started to rephrase her greeting, but Burton had already jumped forward.

"Marsh, one of my network execs, grabbed me this morning after the show and told me your story. Said it was amazing. I agree. You and your mission are inspiring. Brilliant. The whole story is perfect for our show. It's an ideal holiday package segment."

Nonchalant, Hope reminded herself. "What did you have in mind?"

"We'll send a crew to you in the next thirty-six hours. They'll shoot background, interview a few folks, get plenty of tape of people and their jars, do their thing, then in a day or two, we'll fly you to New York to appear live and on-set."

I can be packed in an hour, she thought. "I think I could arrange that."

"Run it by the place, the Chicken people, get permission, round up a few locals, one of my producers will call with details. And make sure Allred is around."

"I sure will," Hope said.

"This is the big time, kid, be ready. Talk soon."

"Uh-huh!"

And just like that Burton Kincaid, senior producer of America's number-one national morning show, delivered the break Hope had been waiting and praying for all year. And he'd hung up before Hope even had time to realize she'd said "uh-huh" and not "good-bye."

"Well?" Clark asked when she finally pried the phone from her ear and hung up.

"I just got the biggest Christmas Jar ever."

After collecting all the money, we gave $1,750 to an orphanage in Tanzania that our school has worked with. Plus $572 each to three families.
—Rachel

TWENTY

Al had never been good at math. It didn't help that he hated it, especially when, more than once, he had tried to run his own business. But he was smart enough to know the hotel bill was mounting, even after asking for and receiving a reduced extended-stay rate.

He'd fished a few times for offers to stay with Tracy, but with no success. Tracy's oldest was moving *back* home, his middle child was preparing to *leave* home, and his youngest was taking *over* the home. "I sure got a full house right now," Tracy said.

Plus, Al had to admit it was nice eating a free breakfast each morning and having someone wash his sheets and clean his room.

While Chuck's was buzzing about Hope's phone call, Al was

celebrating his success by lying low—literally—in bed, watching a Christmas movie marathon. He had the sniffles and a persistent headache, and besides, he thought, it might be strategic for Hope to bask in the attention at the diner for a while.

Only Al knew just how much work he'd done to make the phone call happen. He'd schmoozed a receptionist, a production assistant, a booker, a producer, and finally a man so well-known in morning TV he only went by one name: Marsh.

All of Al's carefully placed phone calls and carefully written e-mails with photo attachments of cute kids and jars led to Marsh cornering Burton Kincaid and insisting he book Hope for the undisputed king of morning TV: *America Live*.

Al's day zipped by with movie after movie, most of which he hadn't seen in so long the plots and feelings felt fresh again. *It's a Wonderful Life, A Christmas Story, White Christmas, The Bishop's Wife, The Shop Around the Corner.* By the time the final credits rolled in the late hours of the evening, he realized he hadn't spoken to Queen in two days, and the window to call and check on his ailing friend was closing fast.

"Hello?" Laura answered.

"Hi, it's Al."

"I think I know your voice by now, Al." It was tired banter, but she was genuinely glad to hear from him anyway.

"It's late, I'm sorry. I'll try again tomorrow."

"No, don't hang up. Queen wants to talk to you."

"She does?"

"Of course. It's been a couple days."

"How is she?"

But before Laura could answer, or even hear the question, she'd given the phone to Queen.

"Ross residence, Queen speaking." Her voice was dull and indifferent.

"You're a silly kid. You don't have to say that when your mother hands you the phone."

"I know," she said. "I was being funny."

Al turned off the television and laid back diagonally across his bed, his head on a pillow.

"How are you feeling today?"

"OK. I'm tired."

"I know it's late there. I'm sorry. I just wanted to check in on my mail."

Queen stayed silent. "You don't have to say that anymore."

"What do you mean?" But Al knew exactly what she meant.

"You can just say you wanted to check on me."

Al covered his eyes. "You're right. May I try again?"

"OK."

"How are you Queen Lara?"

"Still tired."

Al laughed despite the odd lump in his throat.

"You're zonked," he said. "I'm going to say good night and call another time."

"Please don't hang up."

"Alright, Queen. Just a few minutes though. What should we talk about tonight?"

"Twenty Questions."

"You want to play Twenty Questions?"

"Mom and me play a lot. She says it's good for me."

"Alright then. I'll ask the questions. Is that good?"

"Uh-huh."

"Number one. Did you go to the park today?"

"No." She added a dramatic sigh.

"I'm sorry. Number two. Did you notice if the doctor called your mother today?"

"I don't think so. But Mom held the phone all day. And she cried buckets."

Al said "I'm sorry" again, but not loud enough for anyone but him to hear. "Number three. What's your favorite brownie?"

"All of them."

"Agreed," Al said. "All your mother's brownies are good, aren't they?"

"Uh-huh."

"Number four. What's your favorite holiday?"

"Christmas. And sometimes my birthday." Queen's voice was even quieter. "Mostly Christmas."

"Number five. What would you like for Christmas *this* year?"

"A new heart."

Al couldn't recall the last time three simple words had sucked the air from his chest.

"I want that for you, too. Should we stop playing the game?"

"No." She answered so softly Al could barely hear her weary voice brush his ear.

"Alright then. Number six. Let's see . . . Who is your hero?"

Al suspected the pause didn't have a thing to do with trying to decide.

"Mom," she said resolutely.

"I thought so. . . . Number seven. If you could do anything fun this weekend, anything special at all, what would it be?"

"Go for a ride."

"A ride?"

"In the Cluck Truck."

"Great answer!" Al chuckled both at the thought of Queen riding shotgun as they cruised the streets of Idaho Falls and that she'd even remembered the Cluck Truck.

"Number eight. Now that we know how you'd get there, how about the one place you'd visit that you've never been before. Where would it be?"

Finally a question Queen had to consider. Al stared at the ceiling silently trying to predict her response.

"Can I pick two?" she finally answered.

"Of course you can."

"Then New York City." She took a long breath. "And the manger."

"The manger?"

"Where Jesus was born."

"Oh."

Suddenly Al felt compelled to ask, "Number nine. Will you still give me your Christmas Jar when I get home?"

She didn't answer.

"Queen?"

"Yes. I'll give it to you."

Al sat up. "It's late. You need to sleep."

"One more?"

"Alright. Last question. Number ten—and let's give you a stumper. . . . Hmmm. . . . Queen Lara Ross, who—and it can be anyone—would you most like to meet face-to-face?"

There wasn't a moment of hesitation.

"God."

*As she took the jar from my hands, we both wiped
away tears. It was one of the best, most unforgettable moments
of my life. I am committed to keeping the Christmas
Jar going for as long as I live.*
—Georgina

TWENTY-ONE

No one could remember this much excitement at Chuck's
Chicken 'n' Biscuits since Chuck had been named grand mar-
shal of the county Christmas parade a decade earlier.

Gayle was calmly straightening the Christmas decorations
and strategically placing jars around the diner so there wouldn't
be a single camera shot without at least one glimmering jar in
the background.

Mike and Joel were sweeping the parking lot and washing
the outside windows.

Randall and another cook were spit-shining the kitchen and
making sure the overhead fans were pumping the smell of hot,
southern-fried chicken into the dining room. Randall also had
added an extra ounce or two of cream into the pie filling.

Hannah was working as a waitress, something she'd not

done since college, and Lauren was home with a house full of grandchildren.

Clark sat parked in his truck two miles down U.S. Highway 4 on the lookout.

Hope stood outside the diner on the phone. "I know," she said for the seventeenth time, "it's unbelievable."

"I'm so sad I'm not there with you," Marianne said.

"It's fine. Aren't you having the time of your life?"

"And then some," she answered. "This is unlike any place I've ever been. Of course. Books don't do it right, Hope. You have to be here."

"And I'm glad you are. Truly."

"So what time are you expecting them?"

"Anytime. Clark's down the street watching out so we get a little heads up. Did I tell you the producer said they're bringing *two* cameras?"

"You did."

"I'll try not to be in every shot for this piece since they're flying me to New York for a live interview when the piece runs."

"That makes sense, dear."

"Do you know what could come of this?"

"The sky's the limit, Hope, it really is."

"I know, right?"

"Who else is there today?"

"The gang's all here, for sure. They're excited. And Al's here, of course, doing his thing,"

Marianne paused. "His thing? What's his thing, exactly?"

"Oh, you know—organizing, giving ideas. Making phone calls. This interview wouldn't be happening without Al pulling some strings."

"Interesting."

"Yessiree . . . He's been really helpful, I have to admit."

"You trust him?"

"Sure. Why wouldn't I? He's a bit of a salesman, yeah, but he's committed. I can't complain about that, right?"

"I guess not . . . Oh, boy, I've got to go, the tour bus is leaving. I love you."

"Love you, too. A hug to Nick."

The line went quiet and Hope hung up. *This is the big time,* she thought, blowing warm air into her hands.

"Here we go!" Hannah opened the back door and whistled for Hope's attention. "How do I look?"

But Hope didn't hear the question. She turned and faced her. "How do I look?"

Hannah smiled. "Like a vision."

The network team from New York took control of Chuck's like they were the new owners. They rearranged booths for better shots, shifted pictures from one nail to another, powdered noses without bothering to ask, and used every outlet they could, lighting the diner so bright it could have been Chuck's newest franchise on the sun.

Gayle kept her distance, content to soak in Hope's biggest moment in the national spotlight. She sat at a table with Al as far away from the lights and cameras as possible.

Joel and Mike hovered near the segment producer, determined to protect the image, good reputation, and homegrown feel of Chuck's. No one had crossed their imaginary line just yet, but they were willing to defend it if things became uncomfortable.

The two cameras were set up at opposing angles, focusing on the same front-window booth where Hope had been discovered twenty-five years before. The producer interviewed Mike and Joel, Randall, Hannah, Preacher Longhurst, and even Lili, Chuck's chicken-suit-wearing granddaughter. Lauren arrived late, Hope noticed, but still in time for a turn before the cameras. She spoke of Adam's role in the spreading of the tradition and praised Hope for tastefully taking it to the next level.

While the camera crew was shooting exterior shots of the diner and the famed Cluck Truck, three teachers from the preschool Hope once attended arrived to deliver a total of twenty-four small jars. Known to every child in town as simply Miss Stephanie, Miss Corinda, and Miss Nan, the three dedicated women presented eight jars each. "We trust you," Miss Stephanie said to Hope, "to distribute these to people with the greatest need."

The producer gushed about what "great TV" the teachers had provided to the story.

Gayle was asked three times to go on camera, and the producer made a more compelling case with each request. Eventually Gayle agreed, making a short statement, and finishing with, "But this isn't about me. It's about Hope and the jars. We just give them a headquarters for their work—"

"Ministry," Hope corrected, and the producer liked it so

much he had Hope use the word during her own sit-down interview. She'd planned to anyway.

Everyone agreed Hope shined. She sat for a portion of the questions, but stood without warning to point out the heartfelt letters and news articles on the walls and under the glass countertop. As the cameras rolled, she also posed in front of the Board and explained their mission of 1,001 jars. "A record," she claimed, "for our little unofficial non-profit ministry."

Two hours after descending on Chuck's, the cameras, lights, and boom mics were loaded back into a long rental van. "I think we've got what we need here," the producer said. "Mrs. Maxwell offered to let us swing by and get a few shots of their place. So we're gone."

"I'll come along," Hope said. "Just in case, you know, in case you need anything else from me."

"Sure. Fine." The producer saw Al sitting at Gayle's table. "Why don't you come too?"

"I'd love to," Al answered, and before the words had traveled across the diner, he'd risen to his feet and mounted his crutches.

Hope stole a look at Gayle, raised her eyebrows, and followed them all out to the parking lot.

"Al, why don't you ride in the van," the producer said. "It'll be a heckuvalot easier to get in and out of with that bum leg."

Al agreed and climbed in.

Hope climbed in too, but not in the van—in her own car. She trailed very closely behind.

TWENTY-TWO

I t took some time, but the excitement in Chuck's eventually trailed off and the diner slowly emptied. Only Gayle remained; she sat at the same table where she'd been all afternoon. In the back, Randall, a dishwasher, and two part-time waitresses finally ate their own late-lunch.

Gayle stared through the window at the field where Chuck's funeral had played out under the giant green tent. So much had happened since his funeral just three weeks earlier, she'd hardly had a moment to relive that afternoon and replay Preacher Longhurst's remarks in her mind.

It's a cliché, she thought, *but the day was more a celebration of life than a day of grief. Just as he wanted.*

As she lost herself under the tent, the television crew's van pulled back into the lot and Gayle watched the producer help

Al step out. He handed Al his crutches, shook his hand, patted him on the back, and then climbed back in the van. They drove off, and Al swung his way in the front door of the diner.

"You're back," Gayle said.

"You're still here."

"Just enjoying the quiet. At last."

"It *is* quiet, isn't it?" Al noticed that, for the first time since his arrival in town, the diner was empty. "I'm an idiot. I should have had them drop me off at the hotel. I wasn't thinking."

"Nonsense. Have a seat and enjoy the quiet for a moment."

He took his same seat from earlier, directly opposite Gayle, but the sun had dipped just enough that the light now drenched Al's chair. He put his crutches in the chair instead and moved around to Gayle's side of the table.

The same Christmas music that had been on repeat all afternoon played in the background.

"What a day, huh?" Al said.

"It was something to behold, that's for sure." She looked at him. "How'd it go at the Maxwell's?"

"Great, I figure. I don't see how the story can go wrong. Hope's a natural on camera, and I'm good with networking and making things click. I think that number over there is going to look small by the time we're done."

"You're confident."

"Of course. These opportunities are so rare in life, I just feel so lucky to have stumbled into this one. Something's happening here, don't you feel it?"

"I suppose I do. Hope certainly appreciates your help lately, even if she forgets to tell you. I know she does."

Al was lost in his own thoughts. He hadn't noticed before just how tired Gayle's eyes were. He wondered if she'd had a full night's sleep since her husband's funeral. "How are you holding up?"

Gayle's eyes brightened a shade. "I'm hanging in there. You're kind to ask. Thank you."

"I had to wonder if you've been lost in the shuffle the last few days." Al looked at the Board across the diner.

Gayle looked away from Al and out the window. "Oh, no, I wouldn't go *that* far."

"Still, you've been so graceful. At least from my view. It must be hard to lose your husband."

Gayle nodded.

"I wish I could have met him. From all I've heard about him he was really something."

"Oh, he was something alright," Gayle said, staring at the Cluck Truck in the parking lot. "It's not losing a *husband* that's hard. It's losing a *best friend*."

"I've never thought of it like that." Despite his many relationships, Al had never had a best friend who was also his girlfriend or fiancée or wife. For Al, best friends were the guys who went with you to games, car shows, and fishing trips. Guys who laughed at your edgy jokes.

"Have you ever been married, Al?"

He hesitated.

"I'm sorry, I shouldn't have asked. That's not my business."

"No, it's fine. I've been married, yes. Just . . . just not very well."

"That's an interesting way to put it," Gayle said with kindness, not judgment, in her voice.

Al took a drink of the same watered-down lemonade he'd left behind. "I don't know. I've been a slow learner, I figure."

"At least you admit that. Most relationships end because one or the other—or both—think they're the ones doing everything perfectly. When the reality is that relationships are meant to be imperfect; at least that's the way Chuck and I saw it. That's what makes a good marriage so wonderful. They don't happen by accident."

"I always figured if it was meant to be it would be natural. You know, it wouldn't take so much work."

Gayle laughed. "Not in my experience. We loved each other, but we worked at it. Constantly. We almost gave up more than once early on."

"Really?"

"Sure. We loved each other dearly. That much we never doubted. But it took work every day. Discussion. Compromise. I teased him when he said this, but after one of our biggest fights—it was about the diner actually—Chuck said we were two rough stones stuck together, plunging down a long, steep and challenging hill, being smoothed and refined as we rolled along together. But it wasn't just life's hill doing the smoothing, it was us."

Al pictured the faces of the women whose hearts he'd won and broken. "I'm afraid more often than not I've been the hill," he said.

Gayle looked at his profile. "We're always hardest on ourselves, Al."

"Hard to believe," he said. "Plenty of people have been plenty hard on me." He hadn't necessarily meant to make the conversation about himself, yet somehow he had. "Maybe if I *had* been harder on myself I would have realized how much better I could have been doing."

Gayle began to reply, but the front door opening startled her.

"Hello," Lauren said.

Gayle stood and hugged her. "I didn't think I'd be seeing you again today."

Lauren looked down at Al. "I just needed a break. The house is full of kids and grandkids, and some kids I'm not sure I even recognize." She looked back at Gayle and smiled. "And I wanted to check on you."

"You're wonderful, but you didn't need to come all the way back over for that."

"We widows have to stick together," Lauren said. "Don't we now?"

Gayle grinned but wasn't nearly comfortable with the term yet.

"How about you two?" Lauren asked, looking down at Al again.

Gayle extended her hands and did a full rotation. "It's a miracle. Quiet at Chuck's. This doesn't happen very often, does it?"

"Not lately," Lauren said.

Al shuffled to his feet. "I should get going. Big day tomorrow."

"Can I give you a ride?" Gayle said.

"No, I'll—"

"How about I run him back?" Lauren offered. "You go home, Gayle, and get some rest. Big couple of days coming."

"You sure? I was thinking maybe I'd visit the cemetery for a moment before dark."

"Wonderful idea," Lauren said. "Go do that. I'll take care of our friend."

Gayle hugged Lauren good-bye and thanked Al for the pleasant conversation. When he said "You're welcome" and extended his hand, Gayle hugged him instead.

Then she pushed through the swinging door into the kitchen to say good-bye to the staff.

"Ready?" Lauren asked Al as she handed him his crutches.

"Uh-huh."

As they pulled off onto the highway and toward Al's temporary home, Lauren asked matter-of-factly, "Can we talk?"

My family received a jar with money in it.
It was just enough to pay an overdue electric bill.
I feel this was a miracle.
—Ashley

TWENTY-THREE

December 23rd

I wish you were here."

"I know you do," Marianne said. "But Hope, truly, what could I do that you're not doing so brilliantly all by yourself?"

"It's not that so much. It's just so exciting. I can barely stand it. I can't wait for you to get home. I have so much to tell you."

"And I can't wait to hear it." Marianne was enjoying her dream honeymoon even more than she ever imagined, but doubts were creeping into the joy. She began to wonder if she'd made a mistake. "Hope, are you being careful with the money?"

"What do you mean?"

"All those jars and all that money. It must be thousands—"

"Oh, it is. Many thousands, I think. We've not counted it and I don't think we will this year, so long as we hit our goal."

"Is the money safe?"

"Of course. It's all at the diner and it's always being watched."

"And you trust everyone?"

"You're kidding, right? Of course we do, silly woman."

Marianne took an extra breath before finishing, "Just be careful, sweetheart. Be sure no one is looking to take advantage of the situation, of all the goodwill."

"I will."

Hope promised to check in again after the interview and reminded Marianne how excited she was that she was living her dream in the Holy Land.

"Be careful," Marianne said.

"You too."

"I love you."

"Me too." Hope hung up. She walked to the wall and looked at the pictures of Louise, replaying another of that morning's phone calls in her mind.

"Everyone was great," the producer had said.

"Really?"

"The footage looks great, Hope. This is going to be a tear-jerking, heartwarming story. Everyone is really amped up here."

"Really?"

"Yes, yes, yes. Oh, and we've got a little surprise for you, too. You'll love it. It's great TV."

"Awesome!"

"And seriously, we're going to blow up that number on your white board."

"I hope you're right."

"I am. See you tomorrow morning in New York. My assistant will call with logistics for your car."

"Car?"

"We're sending a limo."

"Oh, right, of course."

And we're going to blow up that number on your white board. She loved the thought. *And we're going to blow up that number on your white board.*

Hope's stomach was a knot of excitement and anxiety.

"Knock knock." Clark pushed her apartment door open. "You always leave this thing open?"

"I do when I know a cute boy is coming over."

Clark licked his pinkie and ran it across his eyebrow.

"Sit for a minute. I need a couple favors."

"A ride to the airport isn't enough?" he teased.

Hope didn't hear it. She ripped a page from a legal pad and handed it to him. "Just a few things. Some of this is for Hannah, obviously, but she knows most of it already."

Clark read the list silently. "Who's Mrs. Lytton?"

"Another teacher who has some jars to drop off. Only two, but they're loaded. Make sure they get locked up in the office right away. I get nervous with a lot of cash out front."

"You've got jars everywhere, Hope."

"Not with cash in them. When Mrs. Lytton called the diner she said they were *mostly* cash. More cash than coins."

"I didn't know teachers did so well," Clark quipped, but

once again Hope hadn't heard. She'd hopped off the futon and ran into the bedroom. She came back a minute later with a key ring.

"Here's a key. Do you mind coming by tonight and checking the front porch for jars?"

"You're serious?"

"Yeah, I usually get a jar or two."

Alrighty then, his scrunched brow said.

"Don't worry," she mocked. "I always give them away again."

He continued reading the to-do list. "These people I'm calling—you have numbers for them?"

"Not here, I'm afraid. They're on my desk at the newspaper. Maybe you could run there and pick them up?"

"Sure."

"It's a simple call. We're just reminding them that we're coming by tomorrow night with jars." She took the list back from him. "This one," she pointed, "at the group home—he's the only one who'll be surprised. I didn't even know he existed until I got the tip. He's *way* off the grid, but they can use the jars. We're planning on giving them quite a few."

"Cool," Clark said and kept reading.

"Oh, scratch that one off, Hannah said she would record the interview for me."

"Good," Clark said. "I think I'm busy then anyway. I was hoping someone would—"

"You're not watching it?" Hope whacked him with a throw pillow.

"On second thought—"

Hope looked at her watch and jumped to her feet. "Yow! Let's go."

Clark picked up her bags—one carry-on and one to check—and walked out of the apartment and down to his truck.

Back upstairs Hope took one more look at a photo of her and Louise. "I wish you were here, Mother. You would have loved all this." Hope kissed her hand and touched her mother's face. "Wish me luck."

For the first few miles, Hope mumbled things she hoped she remembered and Clark listened to current country singers sing Christmas classics on the radio. Hope also practiced a few answers to questions she expected she'd be asked during her interview the next morning.

"Why the big goal?" Hope asked her reflection in the window. "Why not?" she answered.

Clark shook his head. "You're a mess."

"Huh?"

"You're nervous. I wouldn't have expected it from you."

"Maybe a little. But not about the interview. About the number."

"It is a *big* number, Hope. Maybe too big?"

"No. It's a *huge* number. That's why we picked it. It's nothing anyone has ever done before. It's a milestone that means next year we could organize even better, get our marketing going earlier—"

"Marketing?"

"You know what I mean—PR, getting the word out. Maybe partner up with a bank. Al actually thought about it for this year but it was too late."

Clark turned off the radio and took Hope's hand.

"Hey, I know I'm the novice here, but isn't Uncle Adam's tradition more about giving one jar at a time and not necessarily about corporate sponsorship?" It only took a glance at Hope's silhouette for Clark to regret the words.

"How many jars have *you* given away?" Hope asked with surprising edge.

"Hold on, I'm not—"

"How many?" Hope pulled her hand away, and Clark pulled off to the side of the road.

"I've been out with my parents a few times. What's the point?"

"The point is, that over the last few years I've personally given away dozens and orchestrated hundreds—"

"Orchestrated?" Clark broke in.

"Come on, you know what I mean. Lauren, Gayle, Hannah, the others. This is what we *do*. We gather jars from people who don't want to give them away themselves, or who need help doing it right—"

"Doing it *right?*"

"There's a way, yeah, and I like to think we've got it down pretty well."

Clark took her hand again and considered asking whether the tradition had outgrown her, or if *she* had outgrown *it*. Instead he said, "Hope, maybe we don't know each other really well yet. But I hope—sorry—I sincerely *think* we are headed in the right direction. So can I make an observation?"

"*May* I," Hope corrected.

"Always a writer." Clark tried to ease the tension with a smile and a squeeze of her fingers.

Hope stared straight ahead out the truck's windshield.

"I'm a rookie with the, what do you call it, the *ministry*. I'm no expert, I admit that, but as an observer, just knowing what I've seen over the years and heard from Uncle Adam and Aunt Lauren, it's not really some *organized* thing so much, is it? Isn't it more of a there's-no-wrong-way-to-do-it kind of thing? In the big picture, whether you give it away through the diner, or on a big TV show, or whatever—maybe someone just gives it away on a porch on Christmas Eve—it's all the same effect. Right? It's about doing one little piece of good."

Hope spun words through her mind before giving them life. Then she rearranged the thoughts again and said, "Clark, if you live in a small world, yes, you're a thousand and one percent right. But we don't live in a small world. We live in a big one, don't we? With big responsibilities and big expectations and incredibly big opportunities. Al and I know this is one of those opportunities. I can do this."

Clark took a deep breath. He gripped the wheel with both hands, looked over his left shoulder, and then pulled back onto the highway and drove on. Half an hour later they arrived at the airport.

Hope hadn't even noticed the tension. She hopped out, kissed him on the cheek, and said, "Wish me luck!"

"You don't need luck, Hope."

Walking backward, she blew him a kiss and said "Good-bye" a final time.

"Good-bye," he whispered as he watched her walk boldly through the automatic doors.

*It wasn't what I had planned for the jar,
but we know it made this young soldier's Christmas Eve
as he tried to get home.*
—Kerri

TWENTY-FOUR

December 24th

Al hadn't slept well for the first time since checking in to the Best Western. He'd not gotten an answer the night before at Queen and Laura's apartment, and he'd called every hour or so until finally leaving a message that he hoped hadn't sounded desperate, but knew it probably had.

Also for the first time since beginning his adventure he woke up missing home. He wondered what he'd be doing in his small Idaho Falls apartment on Christmas Eve. He didn't have many friends there, but certainly an invitation would have come for dinner. *Or,* he imagined, *maybe even to spend the entire day with Laura and Queen.*

He turned on the television. It was still too early for *America Live,* but the local news was teasing the big Christmas Eve festivities planned for later that morning.

He muted the TV and imagined how quiet Chuck's must be in the early morning, and how later the excitement would build to a full roar. The gang planned on meeting early for donuts and milk and to finalize the maps and routes. All the jars coming in to the diner had to go somewhere by that evening, and Joel and Mike had been working on a detailed map and routes for the twenty-five-plus drivers who had volunteered to deliver Christmas Jars.

Al wondered what the Board would read that evening at the magic hour. When he'd left the night before, the number was a staggering 805. Jars were everywhere. On shelves in the kitchen. Cluttering the counters. In the same large cartons the original jars had come in. Some, the ones with the most cash or the largest in size, were locked away in Chuck's old office. Al couldn't even imagine how much money was sitting inside the diner.

He knew it was early in Idaho, but he picked up the phone anyway. Nothing. He counted to sixty and tried again. Nothing. He offered an awkward prayer and tried again. Nothing.

Al imagined the options and wished he'd accepted Queen's jar the first time she'd offered it. Or the second. Or the third and final time at the train station.

He bathed, dressed, and hobbled downstairs for breakfast. The television in the lobby was on and *America Live* began. They were already teasing the segment even though Hope's interview was still an hour away. Just before a commercial break, the hosts, Ben and Connie, challenged viewers to start hunting the cabinets for an empty jar.

"Later in this hour we are going to introduce you to a tradition that has changed so many lives, it just might change yours. But first, when we come back, world-renowned trapeze team Mayer and Hoffmann will demonstrate some of their most jaw-dropping daredevil moves, live from Vegas. Stay with us."

Al remembered his jar on the desk upstairs in his hotel room and wished it were full. He sat for the trapeze segment and then rushed upstairs during the commercials.

At the diner, Gayle, Lauren, and the Christmas Jars family gathered around a television Randall had set up on the lunch counter. When he realized it was too low for everyone to see it clearly, Randall sat on the counter and rested the small television on his broad left shoulder.

Clark watched *America Live* alone from the Maxwell's living room. He sat in Adam's old chair, the very place his late-uncle had shared and trusted their Christmas Jars secret with Hope—the eager young college student.

When the last commercial ended and blended into the show's catchy theme song, Hannah said, "It's time! I'm calling Marianne." She dialed the diner's cordless phone and, after a quick hello, held the phone up to the tiny speaker on the side of the television.

"We've been teasing them all morning, haven't we, Ben?" Bubbly and telegenic Connie said to her co-host.

"Indeed we have. And the wait is over." The camera closed

in on Ben's serious face. "A few days ago we sent a crew to a little greasy spoon with a big heart. The chicken, they say, is fantastic, but their story is even more amazing. Watch."

Ben's emotional face faded to an exterior shot of Chuck's Chicken 'n' Biscuits.

"Wooooooooooo!" They shouted inside Chuck's.

Al sat on the edge of his bed, eighteen inches from the huge television, and shook his head.

Clark smiled from Adam's old recliner.

A baritone-voiced announcer began to tell the story of a diner and a woman on a mission. They cut to short clips of Lauren, Hannah, Preacher Longhurst, and others. Gayle got in a few quotes too, mostly of how supportive her late-husband had been of the Christmas Jars movement.

They showed a picture of Gayle and Chuck holding a Christmas Jar and standing by the register. Tears filled Gayle's eyes almost instantly and Lauren pulled her close.

While the announcer explained the tradition, viewers watched more footage of inside the diner. Close-ups on letters, jars, and newspaper clippings. The announcer even referenced Hope's unusual entry into the world.

"There was a letter," the announcer said. "It read, 'She is yours now. I'll miss her more than you know. But I love her too much to raise her with a daddy that hits. Truth is, he didn't even want me to have her anyways.'"

Gayle's eyes weren't the only ones filled with tears.

The taped story ended and one of the four in-studio cameras went live with a tight shot of Ben and Connie.

"How have we not heard of this before today?" Connie asked her co-host.

"I have no idea. Because this is something that could *literally* change a life. And in fact, it's changed at least *one* life—the life of our very special guest." The camera pulled back to reveal Hope smiling in a chair to the right of Ben.

"Woooooooooo!" They shouted again at Chuck's. "That's our girl!" someone yelled over the noise.

Al smiled and felt the strangest sense of pride for a young woman he hardly knew.

Clark sat forward in his chair. Hope was certainly beautiful in person, but somehow the television made her even more stunning. Clark admired her red dress and matching shoes, but it was her smile the camera loved most.

"Hope Jensen, welcome to *America Live*."

"Ahhhhhhhhhh!" Marianne screamed into the phone. But no one except Nick and half of Jerusalem's residents heard.

Hope sat straight with her hands folded daintily in her lap. "Thanks for having me, Ben. It's an honor."

"The honor is ours, Hope," Connie said. "Now tell us, how did all this happen?"

Hope began her story, repeating some of the details from the taped piece, but revealing new snippets as she wove the tale she'd rehearsed, one she felt confident would inspire a universe of jars. She referenced their goal three different times and explained how much work she'd put into reaching it.

The crowd at Chuck's watched quietly, soaking in every second of Hope's breakthrough moment and not quibbling a bit with the occasional exaggeration or minor omission.

After a few more questions, Ben tossed the show to commercial. "When we come back, a surprise for Hope and a challenge for you, friends, to make this a Christmas to remember."

The busy chatter resumed at Chuck's.

Al sat staring at the television and wondering how he'd been so blessed to have landed, even for just a few weeks, in the family of Chuck's. He also wondered if Queen was watching and quickly tried her number. Nothing. He decided after the interview to start calling hospitals.

The *America Live* logo filled the screen and faded to a shot of Ben, Connie, and Hope. "We're back with Hope Jensen, unofficial president and founder of the Christmas Jars Ministry," Connie said.

"Alright, folks, look at the bottom of your screen and jot down this address. This is where you can personally deliver your jars, if you're fortunate enough to live close, or if not, you can *mail* your jars to the same address." Ben turned to Hope. "Because you'd give them away even after Christmas, right?"

"Absolutely," Hope beamed.

"But here we are, the morning of Christmas Eve, and you'll be delivering the jars tonight, right, Hope?" Ben said.

"That's right. I fly home immediately after we're done here.

There is a family of volunteers—thirty, maybe more—all waiting to hit the streets tonight and deliver jars to those in need."

"That's us!" someone yelled at Chuck's.

"Friends"—Connie looked straight at the camera—"if *you* have a jar, it's time to get on a plane, train, bus, donkey, whatever. Get yourself and your jar to Chuck's *today.*"

"Do you remember how many you needed to reach your goal of a thousand and one jars?" Ben asked.

"When I left, the Board—that's what we call the giant white board on the wall at Chuck's—said eight hundred and five."

"Eight hundred and five. We can do better that that, can't we America?" It was Ben's turn to make his plea as he looked into the camera and repeated Connie's challenge. "Why not a thousand and one? Better yet, why not ten thousand and one? Or a million!" Even Connie thought Ben was beginning to sound more like a televangelist than a morning-show host.

"Hope," Connie said, returning to the script, "before you go, we have a little surprise for you. We didn't have time to fill our own jar here at *America Live,* but we couldn't let you leave empty-handed."

Ben watched Connie earnestly. "She's right." Ben looked back at the camera. "If you were watching a few days ago, you know we asked for people who'd received a jar, or even given one away, to contact us with their stories. We had *so many* calls, Hope. More than we expected."

Connie rolled with the rhythm of the well-choreographed moment. "But one call stood out, didn't it, Ben?"

The camera pulled back and a little girl and her mother walked onstage.

Hope, Ben, and Connie stood.

Al stood, too, and inched even closer to the television.

Clark also rose to his feet in the Maxwell's living room and took a step closer to the television.

"Meet Lara and Laura Ross." Lara carried a familiar-looking jar and wore a tiny lapel mic.

A stagehand put two stools next to Hope. "Hi, there," Hope said and put her hand on Lara's knee as they sat.

"You can call me Queen," she whispered loud enough that viewers could hear.

Ben stood up and walked behind Queen's stool to put his hands dramatically on her shoulders. "That's right, my mistake, dear, your mother told us backstage you prefer Queen."

"I love it," Connie gushed, now standing at Ben's side.

"Queen, your mother here says you want to do the talking, is that right?"

"Yes, sir. Mom says I like to talk a lot."

The adults onstage laughed.

Ben continued, "You have a very special story, Queen. Would you like to tell it?"

"Yes, sir." The camera slowly tightened in on Queen.

Al thought that at that very moment, she actually *looked* like a queen.

Ten million viewers around the country thought the exact same thing.

"My name is Lara. L-a-r-a. There's no *u* sound. But my mother calls me Queen Lara. Or Queen. Or sometimes Lara Q."

Queen's mother was fighting tears already. She clutched a white handkerchief.

"I've gotten a lot of jars. This year I've already gotten *five*. One at school. Two at my mom's job—she has two jobs, that's why—and two at home by our door."

"My, my. That's just wonderful. Lots of people love you, don't they?" Ben didn't wait for an answer. "Tell us about *this* jar and why it's so special."

"It's special because it's *our* jar." Queen looked at her mother. "This is the jar we've been putting all our money in ever since last Christmas." She gave it a shake. "It's pretty full!"

"So cute." Connie noticed Ben's hands were no longer on Queen's shoulders, so she made claim to one and gave her a gentle pat.

"Not that long ago I saw a man break his leg. He fell down some stairs where we live and his leg was broken into so many pieces they had to screw them all back together. I saw the whole thing. And I felt really bad."

"Why did you feel bad, sweetie?" Connie asked.

"Probably because I saw the whole thing. It hurt. He was hurt really bad . . . By the way, his name is Al—he told me I didn't have to call him Mr. Allred. And he's a super good friend now."

Chuck's Chicken 'n' Biscuits became as quiet as it had ever been.

Hope's mouth hung open and the camera noticed.

"And?" Ben asked.

"Al wouldn't take it. He said he didn't need our jar. But I think he does. Even if he doesn't need all the coins inside."

Hope finally closed her mouth. She couldn't believe how dry her lips suddenly were.

"What Queen didn't really want us to talk about, but it's a crucial part of her inspirational story, is that she needs all the jars she can get because you need a new heart, don't you, dear?"

Queen gave Connie a squinty-eyed glare. "Yes," she sneered and her mother snickered.

Ben took over. "Queen is being humble, but, friends, she was born with congenital heart disease. She's been on the transplant list for some time, too long, and is anxiously awaiting a new heart. I've never met a stronger little girl in my entire life."

You have no idea, Al thought.

Queen jumped into the empty, awkward moment they'd created for her. "This is our Christmas Jar," she said again and held it up; the camera zoomed in. "We tried to give it to Al, but like I said, he thinks other people needed it more. So we tried to give it to him again, and he put it back on our front porch. My mom even made him brownies—"

The adults laughed again, except for Hope, who was wishing she'd thought to bring Kleenex onstage.

"He kept giving it back. It made me sad. We liked all the jars the nice people gave us, but we want to give one away, too."

Queen's mother slid off her stool and stood next to her daughter, who continued the story. "My friend Al made me a promise that if I didn't go anywhere, he would accept my jar when he got home to Idaho Falls."

"Where did he go?" Ben asked eagerly.

Queen looked at Hope.

Tears began to fall from Hope's eyes and her once magazine-perfect mascara bled.

Ben filled the dead air. "If your friend won't take the jar, maybe Hope would take it home and add it to her project? You could give it to her right now, and ask all the moms and dads watching right now to also help Hope meet her goal. What do you think?"

Queen looked at Hope, then her mother, then the camera. "No." She wiggled her fingers, motioning for Hope to lean in. "Will you take it to him?"

"Of course," Hope said in a choked whisper.

"Will you give him a super-important message?"

Hope nodded, not because she wanted to, but because she couldn't speak.

"Will you tell him I don't care about a million bazillion jars? I only care about one. *This one.*" She handed the heavy jar to Hope.

Hope nodded again. Tears flowed as freely from Hope's eyes as they had the night she watched her mother Louise die in her arms.

Hope leaned in again, this time to kiss Queen on the cheek. Before pulling away, she whispered something only Queen heard: "*One* jar. *One* birth. *One* Savior."

Queen winked.

Hope's trip home was a blur of airport security, shouts of congratulations from complete strangers, and an emotional phone call with Marianne.

Despite the rush, the journey back to Chuck's provided ample time for Hope to relive the night she received her first jar and the despair she felt at seeing her apartment broken into and her life scrambled into pieces. The memory became warmer as she recalled the day she discovered jar recipients Kimberly Telford, John Willard, and A.J. Francis, each of whom had written thank-you letters in the newspaper to their anonymous angels.

High above the eastern seaboard, with her head resting against the cool airplane window, she looked down and pictured the morning she first met Shane Oaks, the sweet and weary single father who'd given her the final piece of the puzzle that had led her to the Maxwells at 316 Oakliegh Hill. She recalled how badly he'd not wanted to spoil the magic of anonymity.

Then Hope wondered, as she had countless times before, whether Adam would have approved of her article in the paper that launched the life she now led.

It was still dark but nearing dawn by the time she walked in the front door at Chuck's. Despite her careful planning and calculations that she'd be home in time to help deliver the jars, time and the distance to New York had not cooperated. There wasn't a single jar in sight. The army of volunteers were already in their cars and vans, circling town and delivering jars to widows, the homeless, and the unemployed, to churches, to homes for troubled boys, and to any other random recipients who might be in need. Even the Cluck Truck was gone, no doubt filled with jars destined for homes that would never be the same again.

Hope's eyes instinctively went to the wall that had proudly held the Board for so long. Her stomach flipped and she shut her eyes tight, afraid to look. *It has lied to me for weeks,* she thought. *No, maybe I lied to it.*

She turned away and opened her eyes. The Board had been the one thing that drove her above all else. In the holiday's faithful moments that lifted and held her above the loneliness, the Board had been a friend and partner.

Now she didn't care how big the number was.

A noise in the kitchen startled her. But as she walked toward the swinging door, a voice from behind stopped her.

"It's just Randall back there," the voice said.

Hope turned to see Al sitting alone with a basket of tater tots and a tic-tac-toe board.

"Sit with me," he said.

Hope did, and the blurry cloud of her harried Christmas Eve vanished before her faster than a late-March snowfall.

Al replayed his side of their day. The pride he and the rest of her Christmas Jars family felt while watching the interview. The tears they shed. His regret at refusing Queen's gift not once, not twice, but three times.

Hope stopped him and pulled a jar from her carry-on bag. She slid it across the table. "Queen said it's not about a bazillion jars. It's only about one. *This one.*"

Al pulled the jar close to his chest. He leaned down and kissed the lid. "You don't know me, Hope, but I've been a real heel most of my life. I've never cared for anyone very well but myself. And I'm ashamed of this more than anything—but I've always doubted God could ever love a man like me."

"Al—" Hope reached across the table for his hand.

"Wait. This is important." He sat back and rubbed his eyes. "I've been a bad boyfriend, a bad brother, and an especially bad husband."

Randall began to push through the swinging door, but when he saw the scene unfolding, he quickly turned around.

Al waited for the swinging door to swivel to a stop. "Some lessons take a long time to learn, Hope. I figure that's OK sometimes, so long as we know that while we're being too stubborn to learn the lesson life's trying so hard to teach us, some opportunities might come and go. It's wonderful, a miracle really, when we finally do learn those tough lessons. But it's a mixed bag, isn't it? Because sometimes it's a tragedy when we finally realize what came and went while we kept our eyes and heart shut."

Hope sat a little straighter.

"Love isn't perfect, Hope. All those people who say true love is effortless are selling snake oil. And my goodness, anyone who tells you that true love means never having to say you're sorry wouldn't know true love if it hit 'em with a baseball bat."

Hope chuckled.

"Lasting love—the kind that starts with flutters in your stomach and leads you fifty years later to a wooden rocking chair, drinking lemonade on a porch together—well, that takes real work. And a whole lot of forgiveness."

He pushed the tater tots aside and took Hope's hands in his. "And now I figure I finally know what brought me here, the real reason I came. To look you in the eyes and say . . . I'm sorry for not accepting Queen's jar. And I'm sorry for trying to make this, this tiny miracle, more than it should have been. A thousand jars, a million jars—Queen's right. It's about the single jar we give and the single jar we accept."

Hope nodded and a truck pulled into the parking lot and shined its headlights on the diner's front window. Hope hadn't yet looked to see who was behind the wheel, but she prayed it was a newly retired semipro baseball player.

Why me? I couldn't believe someone would want to help me with a Christmas Jar. I knew at that moment my life had changed. I wanted to use the Christmas Jar tradition to help touch many more lives in the future. This is a miracle that will live on long after I am gone.

—Cameron

TWENTY-FIVE

December 25th

Al and Hope looked out into the parking lot as the sky started to break and light bravely began filling the air around them.

There sat Clark, perched in the front seat of the Cluck Truck.

Al hugged Hope and said good-bye before she had a chance to convince him otherwise. As he swung smoothly on his crutches toward the front door, he called back to her, "One more thing. Hope, will you thank Lauren for me?"

"For what?"

"Good advice," Al answered and marched out to the driver's side of the Cluck Truck.

Clark stepped out, stretched in the crisp morning air, and shook Al's hand firmly.

"Do you think I could borrow this?" Al asked. "I promise I'll bring it back."

Clark's smile was the only answer Al needed.

Clark helped him into the truck, loaded his crutches and Christmas Jar on the other side, and waved good-bye. Al rolled out of the parking lot, but before the truck disappeared entirely, Clark heard the distinctive sound of the only horn ever manufactured that went "buck buck."

Al swung by his hotel to grab what little mattered, and drove out of town on a trail for the cold, windy town he couldn't wait to see again: home.

Outside Chuck's diner, Clark turned toward the front window and saw Hope sitting in the booth that knew her best.

Clark slid into the opposite side of the booth and set an empty jar between them.

"Hello there," Clark said, but Hope's eyes were locked on the tabletop. "Hope—"

"Please don't." Hope finally looked up. "I'm embarrassed." She looked down again. "And ashamed."

"Don't be. I'm the one who should be apologizing."

Hope finally made eye contact. "For what?"

"For judging. For pretending to know more than I possibly could have." He opened his hands on the table and motioned for her to place hers in his.

She did. "I'm sorry too. I've been a terrible steward of Adam's tradition. I lost sight of what mattered and I'm afraid I let him down." She pointed heavenward. "And Him, too."

"Not at all," Clark said. "I am proud to report that I have discovered the origin of the Christmas Jar. It was a miracle, nothing less, performed by a child, and today made available to all."

Hope gasped. "You read it?"

"Of course."

She squeezed Clark's hands with hers.

"And you were right. I've never given a jar away." Clark put a finger to her lips to preempt a debate.

Hope smiled.

"But look at me now. Here I am. Sitting before you with a jar. It's not much, but it's my entire offering."

Hope looked down. "It's empty."

"I know. I want to fill it with you."

Hope pulled her hands away and wiped her eyes.

"And you're wrong about one thing." Clark said. "It's not empty."

Hope giggled through a burst of tears and lifted the jar to turn it over. Something fell out and tinged across the table, tumbling to a stop in front of her.

She picked up a bubblegum-machine ring with a tiny plastic chicken where the diamond should be.

She put it on and wiped her eyes again.

"Hope Jensen, will you be engaged to consider being properly engaged to me at a later date?"

She laughed. "Yes now. Yes then. Yes whenever."

Clark leaned over to the midpoint of the table and waited for her to meet him.

She did, and as their lips edged closer, Clark said, "What better place for our first kiss than the altar of Chuck's."

After a long first kiss as a couple engaged-to-be-engaged, Clark whispered, "Have you seen the number yet?"

Hope shut her eyes and shook her head. "It doesn't matter anymore."

But Clark placed his index finger on her chin and tenderly swiveled her head toward the Board. "Yes, it does."

Her eyes were filling with tears by the time she processed the number so carefully drawn in red marker and circled in green.

One.

EPILOGUE

It was after 6:00 PM before she finally woke up. The sun had not yet set and the room was bathed in the soft, recovering light of early spring.

They'd been watching her sleep peacefully for hours. Anxious for her eyes to open. Anxious for a future.

She had visitors on either side of her bed.

One held her hand and prayed quietly. She wore jeans and the same blouse she'd been in for two days.

The other held his own hands, wringing them tightly and looking back and forth between her face and the monitors. He wore slacks and a tan polo with a logo embroidered on the breast pocket that said "Laura's Brownies."

She turned her head to the side and tried to process the faces and the thankful smiles. But before recognizing any of the curious eyes, she noticed something quite familiar and very comforting. Jars, hundreds of jars, sitting humbly like flower arrangements and filling nearly every pocket of space in the otherwise drab hospital room.

But only one jar came into focus. Sitting on a thin table next to her bed she saw a Christmas Jar she knew very well, filled to the brim with coins she'd once put there herself.

An unshaven face slowly appeared in view. "Hello there, Queen."

(June 24)—We're officially halfway to another Christmas!

For most of you, there is probably relief that the busy days and over-scheduled nights are still five months away. The Christmas shopping, holiday baking, more shopping, gift-wrapping, office parties, and even more last-minute shopping are today hidden at the back of your life's closet.

For me, the "Christmas Jar Lady" as some of you now address me in your e-mails and letters, you know I can't wait to get back to December. This year there are things I want to do better.

As my regular readers know, it was an eventful year for this columnist and her friends at her home-away-from-home, Chuck's Chicken 'n' Biscuits on U.S. Highway 4. I've written many times of the Christmas Jar tradition, but last year it reached new heights, touched more lives than ever before, and taught me yet another valuable and humbling lesson.

If you know me well, you know humility and I have never been much more than casual acquaintances. I've worked hard, been rewarded for my efforts, and grown rather fond of my abilities and talents in recent years. Call it human nature, call it the Natural Man Syndrome, call it Hope being Hope. Take your pick.

For a woman born in the most humble circumstances and raised by humility's best friend and constant companion, Louise Jensen, my pride is near unforgivable. I cringe when I imagine what my mother would think of the hubris I've displayed in the past. If it is true that our departed loved ones watch down on us, then I am certain my mother's back was turned through much of last year's holiday season.

Looking back with the perfect vision of uh-oh hindsight, my lofty goals and bold ambitions for growing the Christmas Jars tradition weren't the problem. I was. The flaw—my flaw—was that for a brief period I sought to assume ownership of something that's never belonged to me. As I've said in your churches, schools, and community gatherings, the tradition belongs to every one of you who has ever given or received a Christmas Jar.

The miracle of the Christmas Jar has never been about numbers, grand totals, or breaking records. It has always been about a single jar given in a single moment of selfless sacrifice. Is there power in the cumulative effect of our jars? Of course, and I hope that our churches, schools, and communities will continue raising money together. But in that magic moment of delivery, when the needy recipient is overcome with gratitude and love for someone unseen, they don't think of 1,001 lives changed by the power of a jar. They think of one. Just one.

The irony of last year comes in remembering how the Christmas Jar tradition began. Years ago it was a little girl with a pure heart attempting to give a jar to a reluctant recipient. Now almost three decades later it was another little girl with a pure, but dying, heart attempting to give a jar to a reluctant recipient.

It wasn't easy, but both recipients accepted the jars meant for them and them alone, and their lives were never the same. One, a lovely and brave woman, gave her unborn daughter a better chance at life. And the other, forever a changed man, found another chance at love with a Queen and her mother.

In the past six months, many hearts have changed. And most miraculously, just a few days ago, one was replaced completely.

As for my heart, it is finally whole. The man with a blind spot for curveballs finally hit one out of the park, and I will be married to a man with the best hands in the furniture restoration business on July 4th. The ceremony is private, but you, dear readers, are cordially invited to the reception. 5:00 P.M. Where else?

Chuck's Chicken 'n' Biscuits.

DISCUSSION QUESTIONS

1. Hope's goal is an ambitious 1,001 Christmas Jars. What are some of your life-changing goals? Is it always a good thing to reach for the impossible?

2. Chuck's will contained some unusual requirements, including "Keep living." What unusual or personal requests would you make of your family and friends?

3. Both Gayle and Lauren are widows. How do they approach and handle widowhood? Does one woman handle it better than the other? What advice would you give Gayle?

4. Al feels almost compelled to travel to Chuck's Chicken 'n' Biscuits in search of something new and good in his life. Have you ever felt that drive to change something in your life? Did you follow that inner voice? Was the change a good thing?

5. Marianne and Nick are able to enjoy a long-awaited honeymoon and choose to travel to Jerusalem at Christmastime. If you could plan a special trip anywhere in the world, where would you go?

6. One theme of *Christmas Jars Reunion* is fulfilling dreams—both your dreams and the dreams of others. Discuss the dreams of Hope, Al, and Clark. How are they similar? How are they different? Which of them, if any, have their dreams come true?

7. Al and Queen play Twenty Questions. How would you answer some of Al's questions?

    What is your favorite holiday?
    Who is your greatest hero?
    Who would you like to meet face to face?

8. One evening, Clark teaches Hope how to sand down the edges of a wood block (see page 113). How is that moment symbolic of Hope and Clark's relationship? Why would Adam call that process "magical"?

9. Queen wants to give Al her Christmas Jar no matter what, but Al is not always a willing recipient. Have there been times in your life when your gift or offer of service was rejected? Did you try again?

10. Hope learns an important lesson in *Christmas Jars Reunion*. That is, "One jar, one birth, one Savior." What does that message mean to you?

ABOUT THE AUTHOR

J ason F. Wright is the *New York Times* bestselling author of *Christmas Jars, Christmas Jars Reunion,* and *The Wednesday Letters.* He lives with his wife, Kodi, and their four children in the Shenandoah Valley of Virginia.

THE MAGIC OF THE CHRISTMAS JAR–NOW ESPECIALLY FOR CHILDREN